THE OPEN GATES

THURMAN C. PETTY, Jr.

Pacific Press Publishing Association
Boise, Idaho
Oshawa, Ontario, Canada

Unless otherwise noted, all Scripture quotations come from the New International Version.

Edited by Jerry D. Thomas
Designed by Tim Larson
Cover art by Bryant Eastman
Typeset in 10/12 Century Schoolbook

Library of Congress Cataloging-in-Publication Data:
Petty, Thurman, C. Jr., 1940-
    The open gates: from Babylon's ashes—freedom for the Jews / Thurman C. Petty, Jr.
        p.   cm.
    ISBN 0-8163-1059-9
1. Belshazzar—Fiction. 2. Daniel (Biblical character)—Fiction. 3. Cyrus, King of Persia, d. 529 B.C.—Fiction. 4. Jews—History—Babylonian captivity, 598-515 B.C.—Fiction. 5. Bible. O.T.—History of Biblical events—Fiction. I. Title.
PS3566.E894064   1992   91-24331
813'.54—dc20   CIP

92 93 94 95 96 • 5 4 3 2 1

Contents

A Chronology of the Time of Daniel, Nebuchadnezzar, and Media Persia

Years BC	Babylon	Prophets	Major Events
587			-Belshazzar born
586	Nebuchadnezzar	Jeremiah	-Jerusalem destroyed
585			Nabonidus intercedes
584		Daniel	between Media and Lydia
583			
582		=* Ezekiel	-Nebuchadnezzar invades
581		=	Judah after Gedaliah's murder;
580			fights Syria, Ammon, Moab,
579			Egypt.
578			
577			
576			
575			
574			
573			
572			-Fall of Tyre
571			-Nebuchadnezzar's madness begin
570			
569		=*	-Eclipse
568		=	
567			
566			
565			(?)Nebuchadnezzar's last decree
564			about God (Dan. 4)
563			
562			-Nebuchadnezzar dies
561	Amel Marduk		
560			-Belshazzar occupies important
559			government position
558	Neriglissar		-Cyrus becomes king in Anshan
557			-Nabonidus appointed by citizen's
556	Labashi-Marduk (2 months)		committee
555			-Cyrus/Nabonidus treaty
554			
553			
552			Belshazzar becomes coregent
551			Nabonidus begins Tema Campaig
550			Cyrus becomes king of Media
549			Daniel has vision of ch. 7
548	Nabonidus / Belshazzar		-Daniel's vision of ch. 8
547			-Croesus attacks Cappadocia
546			-Cyrus conquers Lydia and
545			Greek cities
544			
543			
542			
541			
540	END OF BABYLON; BEGINNING OF MEDIA-PERSIA		Cyrus attacks Babylon
539			-Handwriting on wall/fall of Baby
538	Darius / Cyrus		-(?) Lions' den
537			
536			
535			
534			
533			

*Ending dates of prophets' ministries not known.

Chapter 1

The Gathering Storm

"Gobryas!" cried Belshazzar, stumbling down the steps of the throne. "How do you know? I thought Cyrus led the Persian army."

"And s-so did the general." The frightened page fell back in terror, for the king's son had absolute power in Nabonidus's absence. "But the Gutiumite b-banner waves above the commander's ch-chariot."

Belshazzar turned pale. He feared the governor of Gutium (Elam) more than anyone else on earth. Without another word, he dashed from the throne room, called for his horse, and galloped through the Ishtar Gate toward the north outer wall. His bodyguards stumbled all over themselves in their efforts to keep up.

Taking the steps two at a time, he soon scanned the approaching enemy horde. Cavalry led, overspreading the road, steeds prancing, riders sitting bolt upright. Behind them rumbled hundreds of battle chariots, drawn by two or four horses—each vehicle carrying a driver and from one to four archer/spearmen. The infantry followed in battle armor, with shields of leather stretched over lightweight thongs—some overlaid with thin sheets of polished brass or copper. Last came the supply wagons and a multitude of camp followers—

cooks, attendants, wives, and female servants.

Power emanated from the immensity of the army and the arrogance of well-organized fighting men. Brilliant banners flickered above proud platoons, suspended from spears held aloft by elite corpsmen.

But Belshazzar's eyes focused on the gold-plated chariot near the center of the multitude. Dwarfing all others and pulled by six white stallions, the vehicle had a fringed canopy and displayed carvings of cult symbols and previous victorious battles. Gobryas, in colorful battle dress, stood ramrod straight—with dozens of guards, servants, and pages riding nearby.

The king's son had no doubts now. His personal enemy approached with an army capable of taking any city. Retribution had come, and he trembled with terror.

Seeking to hide his fright, Belshazzar began to laugh. "Who do the Persians think they are?" he roared. "Babylon has unscalable walls, unbreakable gates. They couldn't conquer us in twenty years."

"General!" he called as he turned to leave. "Don't get bored watching that exercise in futility. Ha! They'll never get in here." With that he returned to the palace and lost himself in a bottle of wine.

Babylon's strength didn't lie in its walls or well-trained-and-equipped army, but in the caliber of its leaders. The city had lived more than a thousand years, and for most of that time had been the pawn of other powerful nations.

Nebuchadnezzar lifted Babylon to a height she had never known before and had conquered or controlled most of the Eastern world. He ruled with an iron hand, and yet his citizens profited from his justice and benevolence.

Nebuchadnezzar had defeated the Jews and transported them—along with many other conquered peoples—to Babylonia. Most of them had better conditions in the land of their exile than they'd had in their own countries. They bought land and businesses and prospered during their captivity.

After Nebuchadnezzar died, his son Amel-Marduk took the throne. He showed kindness to the Jews by freeing King

Jehoiachin. The now-graying monarch had spent thirty-seven years in prison. The new king provided him with a house for his family and issued him food and clothing to meet his needs.

For all his kindness, Nebuchadnezzar's son lacked wisdom and administrative skill. Babylonians seldom forgave inefficiency in their kings, and unrest brewed. After only two years, he died at the hands of his brother-in-law Nergal-shar-usur.

The Jews trembled when Nergal-shar-usur took the throne, for he had commanded Nebuchadnezzar's armies at the final battle against Jerusalem. He had no love for the Hebrews, and their social position suffered during his reign.

An old man when he took the throne, Nergal-shar-usur's health soon began to deteriorate. His only son, Labashi-Marduk—young and immature—showed neither wisdom nor the ability to rule. The old king feared that the empire might collapse if the boy became king, so he appointed his brother-in-law Nabonidus to follow him.

Nabonidus had good parentage, but he hadn't descended from royal blood. He had no relationship to Nergal-shar-usur, either—except that the two had married daughters of Nebuchadnezzar.

In spite of Nergal-shar-usur's efforts, his foolish son took the throne anyway. Labashi-Marduk exulted that he had overruled his father's will, and he proudly claimed every royal privilege for himself.

He knew nothing of administration or justice, and his supporters soon realized their mistake. Within a year of his coronation, his "friends" took control of the palace guard, arrested the king as a malefactor, and tortured him until he died. Having saved the throne from mindless tyranny, they formed a select committee and appointed Nabonidus to take his place.

★　　　　★　　　　★　　　　★

Nabonidus thanked his lucky stars. He had never dreamed of becoming king of Babylon, but now he enjoyed the privileges of the highest human in the empire. His people worshiped him as god, and he commanded absolute power over the lives of all his subjects.

"It's enough to turn the head of a lesser man," he confided in Nitocris, his wife. "And I'll bet you never thought you'd be queen."

"No," replied the mature, but still beautiful woman as her maid arranged her hair. "Mother was an Egyptian princess before she married Nebuchadnezzar, but he never considered her more than a secondary wife. I'm sure he'd have never married me off to you had he felt otherwise." She laughed at the irony.

Nabonidus grinned. "I suppose not." He ambled over to an ornately carved cupboard built into the wall, retrieved a bottle of fine Babylonian wine, and poured a small portion into a goblet. Then he paced the floor, lost in thought, sipping wine at intervals.

"That poem you recited at the coronation was beautiful," the maid interrupted his thoughts. An older woman, she had lived in their household for many years and had become almost a daughter to them. "Would you say it again?"

Nabonidus's resonant voice echoed through the room.

> Unto the midst of the palace they brought me
>> And all of them cast themselves at my feet,
>> And kissed my feet, and paid homage to my royalty.
> At the command of Marduk, my lord,
>> I was raised to the sovereignty of the land,
>> While they exclaimed, "Father of the land!"
> I do not have an equal!

"Bravo!" the maid cried as she bowed before her master, her forehead touching the floor. "May my lord rule long and prosper." Nabonidus smiled at her and stopped in front of the window, staring into the garden. He watched as an elderly man bent over to sniff the rose blossoms. That's Daniel, he thought. He must still be a member of the royal advisors.

Years ago he had watched from this same window while Nebuchadnezzar ate grass like an ox. He and Nitocris had marveled at the kindness of this Jewish captive and the power of his God in humbling the god-king of Babylon.

The king's mind wandered. What lies ahead? he wondered. Why did they choose me? One of the generals could have ruled with a strong hand. Why did they pick me?

He glanced again at his wife, and at once he knew. They chose me because of her. She's the daughter of Nebuchadnezzar, and her son—our son—is the direct heir to the throne.

The thought both pleased and unsettled him. Pleased to be king; unsettled that it hadn't been because of his own merits. Embarrassment swept over him as he wondered how many people knew that he'd been selected only to preserve the kingdom for his firstborn son—Belshazzar.

Nitocris guessed the reason for his silence and rose from her vanity. "Don't fret about our relationship to Nebuchadnezzar," she whispered as she stroked his beard. "Your father was a noble prince, and your mother the most revered priestess of the moon-god Sin. The nobles chose you because you're the most respected man in the kingdom. Remember your diplomatic mission to Lydia?"

How could he forget? Thirty years ago, Media's armies had spent five years fighting warlike tribes from Lydia. They'd begun to fret because the battles had come to a stalemate, so they asked Babylon to help them settle the dispute by mediation. Nebuchadnezzar sent Nabonidus, and the young man had been so successful that the two countries formed an alliance. They sealed their agreement by the marriage of the daughter of Alyattes the Lydian to Astyages the Mede.

"Everyone knows about your part in that agreement," Nitocris continued. "And through the years you've been one of the highest officials in the kingdom."

She clasped her hands behind his neck. "You're not the first to call yourself 'Father of the land.' "

He looked at her in surprise.

"It's true," she went on. "I've heard others call you that. You have no equal, Nabonidus my love." She stood on her toes to kiss his cheek above his curly beard. "For many years, you've been so influential in Babylon that people feel you're the most capable leader they have. That's why they chose you to rule at this critical time."

Nabonidus hugged her so tightly she squealed. "Nitocris," he mumbled as he scooped her up and carried her into their bedchamber, "you know how to stroke an old man's fur."

The maid smiled, closed the curtains, and turned to busy herself in another room.

★   ★   ★   ★

The envoys who stood before Nabonidus had come from a small country north and east of Babylon—a subject state of the great Median empire, called Persia. The king scrutinized them for several minutes before granting them audience. He'd heard that a powerful chieftain was gathering personal support from the various tribes in that area.

Persians had few diplomatic dealings with Babylon, and Nabonidus wondered why Cyrus sought to change that now. At last, he gave the signal and the men came forward. They moved into position, bowed to the floor, and then rose when Nabonidus extended his scepter toward them.

"We represent Cyrus, king of Anshan in Persia," announced the leader. "Our king requests a treaty with you."

"Why would he want a treaty with me?" asked Nabonidus. "We've never had any dealings before." The king had reigned only a few weeks, but his intimate knowledge of government affairs had already aided him in making several important decisions.

"Our lord Cyrus, king of Anshan," continued the envoy, "has a quarrel with Astyages, king of Media, and he wants to settle this argument in a fitting way . . ."

"We've been friends with Media for many years," interrupted Nabonidus, frowning. "Why should we make a treaty that might harm our friends?"

"Your friendship with the Medes has become somewhat fragile in recent years," countered the ambassador. "Your alliance seems more for mutual self-protection than friendship."

"You've watched us closely," observed Nabonidus.

The envoy sighed. "We find it helpful to know our neighbors. Otherwise we might be caught off guard." He crossed his arms, glared at Nabonidus, and spoke in an impatient man-

ner. "Now, if you please, my lord. Cyrus must address a griev-
ance with Media."

Nabonidus smiled at the man's arrogance, but ignored it.
"What do you suggest?"

"His Majesty Cyrus, king of Anshan in Persia, needs your
help. Should he go to war with Media, he asks your pledge
that you will not join the Medes to fight against us."

"I will consider your request." With that, Nabonidus dismissed the delegation.

The Babylonian king pondered Cyrus's proposal. There were
so many details to weigh—his relationship with Media, caravan routes through Persian territory, the effect the treaty
might have on other nations outside his empire. By nightfall he
hadn't yet concluded what to do. So he left it for another day.

During the night he had a dream. The great dragonlike god
Marduk stood before him. "You are to restore the temple of
Sin in Haran," the creature said.

"But that's impossible," objected Nabonidus. "Media con-
trols Haran."

"The Mede of whom you are speaking," answered Marduk,
"he himself, his land, and the kings who march at his side are
not! When the third year comes, the gods will cause Cyrus,
king of Anshan—his little slave—to advance against him with
his small army. He will overthrow the wide-extending Medes;
he will capture Astyages, king of the Medes, and take him
captive to his own land."

When he awoke, Nabonidus told his advisors of the Persian
request and of his dream.

"There's no doubt about it," breathed the chamberlain in
awe. "Marduk wants you to become an ally of Cyrus." He
scratched his head for a moment, thinking. "I don't see anything illegal with their request. They just want us to stay out
of their argument."

"Seems reasonable to me," replied the commanding general.
"We have enough to worry about without sending troops to
Persia."

So Nabonidus drew up a tentative agreement and appointed an ambassador to return with the Persians to Cyrus.

Nabonidus agreed that, should Media and Persia go to war, Babylon's forces would become involved somewhere else.

Shortly afterward, Nabonidus gathered his army and advanced up the Mesopotamian valley. He had little difficulty conquering Haran and the surrounding countryside.

"It won't be long now," he boasted to his general. "Soon I'll repair the temple, and Marduk's decree will be fulfilled." He smiled as another thought graced his mind. "Soon," he added, "my mother will once again be able to carry out her duties as priestess of Sin."

★   ★   ★   ★

The Babylonians liked their new king. As soon as he had taken the hands of Marduk, the unrest of the past six years ended, and people breathed easier. Business flourished, and prices began to stabilize. Crime declined, and bureaucratic corruption—so rampant since the death of Nebuchadnezzar—sank out of sight.

Nabonidus traveled throughout Babylonia, learning the needs of his people and making decisions about their welfare. He commanded that the priests restore the Esagila temple of Babylon to the beauty it had during Nebuchadnezzar's time. He also ordered that they rebuild other temples in the city that had fallen into disrepair.

He made special pilgrimages to temples throughout Babylonia, including that of Sin in Ur, Shamash in Larsa, and Ishtar in Uruk. He gave large donations from the royal treasury to support their services.

Some of the nations Nebuchadnezzar had conquered had taken advantage of the chaotic times since his death and withheld their taxes. Babylon considered this a rebellion against her authority. Nebuchadnezzar would have wasted little time punishing them, but the weak kings had done nothing, and the rebellious "children" wandered at will.

Nabonidus decided he needed to bring these delinquents back under his power so their taxes would help fill his royal treasury. He needed the money now, more than ever, to help pay for the repair work he planned throughout the empire.

The king had no hassle rallying the army to his cause. They yearned to do something more than the police work that had occupied them for the past six years. They showed such enthusiasm that they made their preparations in less time than their leaders expected.

"I'll be back in a few months," Nabonidus consoled Nitocris. "I'm leaving state affairs in the hands of my chamberlain. Keep an eye on him. You can never tell when some official will begin to lust after my throne."

"You still have doubts, don't you?"

Nabonidus frowned. "The last six years have been terrible, my love. Two kings were murdered by their own friends. I can't help wondering, 'When will they come for me?' Perhaps my success as a military man will change all that."

"I hope it changes your feelings about yourself." She put her arms around his chest and gave him a squeeze. "But you can count on me to watch out for you." She looked up into his large brown eyes. "I'll miss you."

He smiled but didn't reply. "Better keep an eye on Belshazzar too," he added. "He's headstrong and likely to get himself into trouble if you don't watch everything he does."

"He has a lot of talent," she objected. "If you'd put him to work, maybe that'd keep him out of mischief."

"I'll think about it." The king bent over and kissed the little princess on the forehead, turned on his heels, and left.

During his first campaign, Nabonidus conquered the country of Hume—the homeland of iron. In the second year, he warred against Hamath, the great city of northern Palestine. He brought its peoples into subjection to his rule and collected large amounts of taxes for his treasury.

On his third campaign into Palestine, he ascended into the mountains of Amananus, renowned for its fruit orchards. He had his men collect large amounts of the fruit, then had it dried and sent back to Babylon—with a special assortment for Nitocris and his harem.

When he returned from this third campaign, the king had taken ill. Some thought he might die, but the physicians and enchanters ministered to him and brought him back to health.

After only a few weeks, Nabonidus returned to the wars, this time marching against Adummu and Shindini. The towns fought bravely, and his army suffered many casualties because of their fierce resistance. When he finally subdued them, he executed their kings—as an example to others who might decide to follow their example.

★   ★   ★   ★

"How is your health, Mother?" Nabonidus embraced the elderly woman.

The old priestess had passed her 100th birthday and, even before her son ascended the throne, she was one of the most famous women in the empire. "My eyesight is keen," she answered, "my hearing excellent. All forms of food and drink agree with me."

"I'm so glad," returned the son.

The king changed the subject as he led his mother into the garden of the ancient holy place. "I want to rebuild the temple of Sin, here in Haran."

"O, my son." The woman stopped and looked up at his aging but still-handsome face. She ran her hand through his salt-and-pepper hair and smiled. "That would be a most wonderful gesture. Sin will be so pleased." She stepped back and smoothed her priestess robes with her hands as she glanced around her. The broken-down buildings and disfigured monuments gave only a glimpse of the glory this sacred place once enjoyed. She had dedicated her whole life to honoring the great god of the moon—and teaching her son to reverence him as well.

"I have in mind building a statue of Sin, in the form of the moon during an eclipse." The king spoke as the two entered an open place between several dilapidated structures. "While repairing the older buildings, I want to construct a new temple right here." He turned slowly as his outstretched finger drew an imaginary circle. "Then we'll erect the image of Sin in front of the new edifice."

For several minutes the two lingered, each visualizing how the holy house and its image would appear, entranced with the thought of doing a great work for their god.

"This will be the most important project in the empire." Nabonidus broke the long silence, staring at the distant hills as he spoke. "None of the other gods will be happy until Sin inhabits his own sanctuary." The glory of the moment and the mellow sound of his own voice reacted upon himself, causing him to make an unwise proclamation. "In honor of Sin, we'll suspend all religious festivals until we complete this temple. We'll even cancel the New Year's celebration—and the Marduk ceremony for renewing the royal mandate."

The old woman glanced at her son in alarm and started to speak, but he put his finger to her lips. "Never mind, Mother," he murmured. "I am Nabonidus, king of Babylon. I will cause all Babylonia to learn the glory of Sin . . . and all mankind shall worship him."

★   ★   ★   ★

"How can we make a treaty with the Arabians?" complained the chamberlain. "They have no central government. They're just independent tribes who can't even get along among themselves."

"Right," agreed the special envoy. "I visited scores of desert chieftains trying to arrange a trade agreement. Many would rather fight than talk. If I hadn't had a sizable bodyguard, I might never have escaped."

"We've got to find some way to guarantee that our merchants can travel safely to Egypt." The treasurer scratched his head. "They can go up through Hattiland [Palestine], of course, but that takes many days longer."

"Some merchants enjoy the effortless journey around Arabia by ship," suggested the admiral.

"That has a lot to recommend it," agreed the financial advisor. "But it takes even longer. The longer it takes, the higher the prices. And the higher the prices . . . ."

"The fewer goods people will buy," put in Nabonidus, "and the lower our economy sinks." He rose and descended the steps, pacing around the room, his counselors in tow. He visualized camel caravans moving relentlessly across the deserts, carrying everything of value upon which his kingdom depended.

"But we're not just talking about Egyptian trade here." He stopped to face his council. "We need to trade with the Arabs ourselves."

"True," chorused the group.

The western half of the Arabian peninsula held extensive gold deposits, often called "the gold of Ophir." Equally important were the spices, frankincense, myrrh, cassia, cinnamon, resinous gum, balsam, and other aromatic products found only in that arid land. Many a traveler had described how the atmosphere seemed to be laden with perfume.

The mountains of central Arabia also yielded precious stones—some found nowhere else in the world. These were in great demand for use in Babylonian temples and palaces.

"One of our leading merchants once told me that Tema commands a central position in 'the island of the Arabs.' " The army commander crossed his arms and raised his nose into the air as he talked, much as a dog sniffs the wind. "It's about halfway to Egypt, you know. If we conquered Tema, we'd control all Arabia."

"And all the caravan routes as well," added the treasurer, pointing his finger at the military man. "Good thinking."

"Hmmm." Nabonidus eyed the two men. "No one has ever campaigned against Arabia," he thought out loud. "Nebuchadnezzar dashed across the peninsula once to guarantee his throne. I've heard him tell how dry and forbidding the country can be." He stroked his beard and squinted at one man, then another, lost in thought.

"How could a major army survive?" He spoke to the general, but the military man knew he hadn't finished. "There's so little water—only oases a day apart. Caravans use camels, but what about 100,000 men and all their horses?"

"My lord." The small man had been on the council for years, but seldom spoke. "When I was young I lived with desert robbers. They had horses; they needed water and found it." He shuffled his feet and looked at the stone pavement. "I say there's enough water for your 100,000 men—and their horses."

"My father crossed the desert with Nebuchadnezzar," added the general. "Many times he told me how they found the water they needed. I think we can do it."

"Sounds good to me," agreed the chamberlain.

"Then let's do it." Nabonidus smiled. "Gentlemen, soon we shall control the most important caravan routes in the world. Soon we'll own earth's finest source of gold."

★   ★   ★   ★

"O Sin," prayed Nabonidus as he knelt with Nitocris and Belshazzar in the moon god's temple at Ur. "Save me from sinning against thy great divinity and grant life unto distant days as a gift." He placed his hand on Belshazzar's shoulder. "Furthermore, as for Belshazzar, the first son proceeding from my loins, place in his heart a fear of thy great divinity and let him not turn to sinning; let him be satisfied with fullness of life."[1]

As the three rose from their worship, Nabonidus spoke to his oldest son. "I'm entrusting you with the kingship of Babylon. You will have command of the homeguard soldiers everywhere in the country. I adjure you to keep the peace, execute justice, and provide for the sustenance of my army in the field."

"Yes, Father."

"Your mother will be your counselor, and my chamberlain will help you in the affairs of state." Nabonidus hesitated. He didn't trust his son. He remembered the young man's crime against Gobryas and knew the perversity of his heart. He hoped that the weight of national responsibility would mature him and make a real man out of him.

"You are to obey all my decrees," continued the older man, "and from time to time I'll send you instructions from the field. I don't expect . . ."

He paused as his eyes fell on Nitocris. How beautiful she is! he thought. I wish I could take her with me. He looked back at Belshazzar and continued: "I don't expect to be gone more than a few months. When I return, I want to find the kingdom as prosperous as when I placed it into your hands."

"Yes, my lord." Belshazzar smiled as he bowed to his father. Inside he gloated with expectation at the power placed in his hands and the opportunities he'd have to advance his social and financial position in Babylon. Yet he felt a nameless dread at the tight reins his father placed upon him.

What if my father becomes dissatisfied with my work? he wondered. Will he then pass over me and choose instead my little brother Nebuchadnezzar? He made a mental note to "take care of" the younger son of Nabonidus. He wanted no rival to his throne. He knew just how to do it too. He'd been successful before in that sort of scheme.

Young Nebuchadnezzar sensed the hatred in his brother's heart. Within hours after Nabonidus marched toward Arabia, the lad fled for his life, disappearing forever from the pages of history.

★   ★   ★   ★

Arabia's arid terrain did not pose an impenetrable barrier between Babylonia and Egypt, and its people had not committed themselves to total isolation. They played a real part in the world.

Arabia's geography, racial mix, and economy closely matched that of Babylonia. Of all the countries of the Westland, it alone bordered on Mesopotamia. Many points of similarity drew the two lands together, and there had been some intermarriage of their peoples.

When Nabonidus launched his campaign to annex Arabia, he knew the story of his efforts would go down in history. The size of his quest staggered him. If successful, he would add a piece of land many times larger than the combined area of the whole Babylonian Empire.

The army moved slowly across the vastness of the desert, stopping at each oasis to replenish its water supply. The men stored the life-sustaining liquid in large sealable pots and in goatskin bags. Soldiers carried their own goatskin "canteens," slung by leather thongs over their shoulders. The army also took many camels to assure a means of transporting supplies in an emergency.

After many weeks of slogging through the hot sand, the great Babylonian war machine rumbled into the wide Tema valley. At an elevation of 3,400 feet, the valley extended from southeast to northwest—about two miles long and four or five hundred yards wide.

Nabonidus gasped and reigned up his horse. For many minutes he sat in the saddle, spellbound by the beauty of the countryside and the ornate workmanship of the town's walls. Flourishing gardens and groves surrounded the tiny city. He could identify peaches, figs, oranges, lemons, barley, and wheat. Myriads of palms throughout the valley suggested dates as the main course on Tema's tables.

"What a beautiful place," exclaimed Nabonidus. "And the air here is so pure."

"I know," agreed his general, who rode beside the king. "What a contrast to the miasmatic atmosphere of Babylonia."

The monarch drew in a long whistle. "I think I could live here forever."

The Temites turned out to be Arameans, not Arabs, and seemed to resemble the Syrians in their speech and culture. Their scouts had spotted the monstrous army approaching, and they had prepared well to defend their city. Walls and turrets bristled with fighting men who fought fiercely, inflicting enormous casualties upon the attacking army. But the Temites couldn't hold out against Nabonidus's seasoned veterans, and the city soon fell.

As Nabonidus directed the onslaught and saw the savagery of the city's defenders, he felt an anger mushroom up within his heart. The long, dry march from Babylon; the sudden beauty of the Tema valley; the unrelenting energy of the defenders; and the more-than-average losses in the attack all combined to distort his sense of mission and justice.

He forgot his purpose to establish allies to protect the trading routes. He forgot his desire to form treaties with the Arabs in order to buy gold and spices for Babylon. His sudden lust to have Tema all for himself merged with his burgeoning rage at the Temites' desperate efforts to keep it. His now-unbalanced mind began to devise a sinister course of action. He wanted no tribute this time: he wanted everything.

Barking commands right and left, Nabonidus wasted the entire population. From the king on the throne to the most miserable beggar in the street, he had them all herded out of the city—men, women, and children. He selected the most beautiful women for his own harem and to give as concubines to the wealthy nobles who accompanied him.

Then he set his army on the rest and watched with satisfaction as an entire civilization perished amidst the screams of the terrified and the dying. Within minutes, the deadly thrusts of Babylonian swords had done their work. Tema's children had become extinct, and their lifeless bodies gathered into heaps for one vast holocaust.

Nabonidus smiled. Now the city belonged to him. Bursting with the pride of personal power, the Babylonian king rode his favorite horse before his cheering troops and through the gates of the now-deserted city—his city.

This will be my base of operation, he thought. From here I'll gain control of the entire peninsula. Arabia will become the crowning jewel of my empire.

---

1. Prayer of Nabonidus from a cuneiform tablet found in Ur.

Chapter 2

Homesick for Jerusalem

"Belrisua," Belshazzar growled. "Bring me a platter of fruit and a goblet of wine."

The servant bowed to the king's son and backed away into an adjoining room. He soon returned with the requested treats.

"Now explain that transaction again, Nabusabitqati. I want to make sure you followed my instructions." Belshazzar never handled business transactions himself. He had his servants execute the details for him, but he always inspected their work to assure that they'd obeyed his orders—to the letter.

The palace steward rankled at the abrasive tone in Belshazzar's voice. He despised the king's son treating him as though he had no intelligence, but he showed no outward emotion. He bowed and began reading from the still-moist clay tablet on which a palace scribe had recorded the contract.

"By the gods Bel, Nabu, the Beltu of Erech and Nana," he droned, "and the decrees of Nabonidus, the king of Babylon, and Belshazzar, his son, they took oath as follows."

Nabusabitqati cleared his throat and continued. "[As to] one mina and sixteen shekels of silver, principal and interest, the claim of Nabusabitqati, the steward of Belshazzar, the son of the king, which [are charged] against Beliddina, the son of

21

Belshumishkun, son of Sintabni, and (for which) the seed field which (is) between the city gates has been taken as a pledge, the money, amounting to one mina and sixteen shekels, Nabusabitqati from Itti Mardukbalatu, the son of Nabuaheiddin, son of Egibi, has received (as a charge) against Beliddina."[1]

"Good." Belshazzar rubbed his hands together and smiled. "The field's worth many times what I loaned him. If he fails to pay, we'll have his land. And," he winked, "we'll see that he defaults—now, won't we?" He laughed as he thought of the fortune he was amassing while serving his father.

Short and stocky, the king's son had a broad nose and eyes that slanted slightly upward at the outside corners. He'd grown up in the lavish home of Nabonidus and had once served as chief officer to King Nergal-shar-usur. Being a descendant of the great Nebuchadnezzar and the grandson of a famous priestess, he was well-known and favored wherever he went. He expected preferential treatment. He was well-educated and knew the mechanics of administration. But he was a spoiled brat.

Belshazzar displayed great zeal in supporting all the famous gods, making pilgrimages, paying tithe, and giving large offerings—all with appropriate fanfare. He enjoyed arguing points of doctrine, often playing devil's advocate and pitting one religion against another. At heart, he followed his father's leanings toward the god, Sin, but he supported other deities when it gave him some political advantage.

The king's son had an intimate knowledge of Nebuchadnezzar's life and of the mental illness during his later years. He'd been in his late teens then, and often watched the animal-man eating grass in the palace garden. His mother had retold the story to him many times. She often read him her father's decree extolling the Most High God, but the young man chafed when he heard it. He convinced himself that Nebuchadnezzar was still insane when he wrote it.

A deep conviction that she was correct lingered in his heart for years, but Belshazzar refused to admit it. Time and again he fought fierce battles with his conscience. "Mother thinks the Jewish God is the greatest," he once confided to a friend. "She says, 'He made proud old Nebuchadnezzar humble.' Rubbish!" he'd shouted, clenching his fists. "Nebuchadnezzar went crazy all by himself. The Jews are no better than anybody else—and Sin can put Yahweh to shame any day."

When Belshazzar came to power, he didn't persecute the Jews openly, yet he made them no concessions either. Whenever he could, he issued decrees that would increase their burdens.

"I detest them," he told his counselors. "They worship a God I don't understand and keep a day that's different from ours." He looked down his nose at his fingernails. "I have broad religious tastes," he gloated, "but I can't swallow their outrageous beliefs."

As Belshazzar's reign progressed, his annoyance turned to hatred. With nothing to check it, his animosity finally blossomed into an open defiance of Yahweh.

"May the king's son live forever." The old man who stood before Belshazzar gave the traditional greeting and bowed to show respect for the monarch's office.

"What do you want, Daniel?" Belshazzar could hardly control his disdain for this man and his God.

Daniel came right to the point. "The Lord God placed you upon the throne of your grandfather Nebuchadnezzar and gave you power over Babylon under your father Nabonidus." He measured each word, speaking in solemn tones. "But you have failed to act according to His will."

Belshazzar's face flushed with anger, and a fire of hatred flamed up within the furnace of his heart. Yet he could find no words to stop his antagonist.

"God hates your crime against the Prince of Gutium," continued Daniel. "He despises your unjust decisions and your false dealings with your own people. All these evils have come up before Him, and He requires that you be punished."

The prophet's voice mellowed. "But Yahweh is merciful. He has granted you time to repent, to turn from your wicked ways. You can still reign in justice and integrity, as your grandfather Nebuchadnezzar did. You can still . . ."

"Enough!" shouted Belshazzar, at last finding his voice. "I don't want your counsel!" He felt a fury take control of his entire being that created an almost uncontrollable desire to kill the hated Jew with his own hands. But he didn't dare. People throughout the empire liked Daniel, and his father would surely call him into account for such a rash act.

Regaining some control, the king's son squinted at Daniel. "We no longer need your services, old man." His tone hung as heavy as ice. "You've outlived your usefulness here. It's time you retired."

"According to your word," replied Daniel, as he started to leave.

"Bow to me, Jew!" shouted Belshazzar.

Daniel turned and smiled. "Out of respect for your father— whom I continue to serve . . ." He tilted his head slightly and left the room.

Belshazzar burned, but others smiled at Daniel's courage.

"My father! My father!" roared the king's son. "Everyone pays homage to my father. I should have become king, not him. I'm the grandson of Nebuchadnezzar—I served as Nergal-shar-usur's chief officer—my father gave the kingship to *me*. Why don't people respect me for *my* position?"

No one answered him. They all secretly rejoiced that Nabonidus still held control and protected them from the tyranny of his son.

The silence brought Belshazzar to his senses. Nabonidus's personal popularity with those in the palace and the army made it possible that this statement could be reported as treason. The king's son felt a bit chagrined.

"Well," he mumbled, loud enough for those who stood nearby to hear, "I guess my father *is* the king after all, isn't he?" He laughed as though he'd done it all as a joke, but his chuckles sounded hollow.

Daniel suffered right along with all the other Jews. In his seventies now, the prophet still enjoyed the full bloom of health. He grieved that the king's son banished him from the palace and had noticed a touch of sarcasm in the royal voice, a satisfaction that he'd put the old "meddler" out to pasture.

Daniel felt hurt by the slur against himself and his God. He remembered Jeremiah's words, "We would have healed Babylon, but she was not healed." Babylon's future would turn out quite differently if she would only accept Nebuchadnezzar's last decree.

The old seer decided to visit the Jewish colony nestled beside the Chebar Canal. As he strode down the main highway, he thought about the status of his fellow Jews.

Life had treated them well in many ways. Some were tenant farmers, while others labored as date growers, fishermen, and goatherds. As the years passed, many had purchased farms or built houses and businesses. They all raised large families. In spite of their successes, though, many Jews felt discouraged. In their minds, Yahweh had failed to save them from the armies of Nebuchadnezzar, and to some this proved that He had no power to protect them at all. Many gave up the faith, married Babylonians, and lost all ties with the Jewish nation.

Others believed that God hadn't forsaken them at all. They accepted the things they couldn't control and clung to the aspects of their religion and culture that set them apart from other peoples.

These Jews gave up their idol worship and started synagogues—houses of worship and education. They taught their children about the history and religion of Israel—the Exodus, the covenant at Mt. Sinai, and the meaning of the messages written by the prophets. They trained the little ones how to keep the Sabbath, how to remain free from ritual defilement, and why God asked them to circumcise their male children and offer blood sacrifices.

During this time, Jewish scholars gathered the writings of the prophets into collections of books. They made copies of these Scriptures and sent them to all the Jewish colonies.

Most of the priests had died during the Jerusalem war. Now the colonists had few anointed men to lead them in their worship. The Levites—from the same tribe, but not members of the priestly families—joined their cousins in teaching religion. This helped to put the synagogues on a firm foundation.

Some priests developed a "holiness code." They insisted on reverence during worship, and that only priests could lead out in sacred services. They offered sacrifices only at the proper times and required the people to follow the rituals and prayers that Moses taught. They also made sure that none of their services resembled the idol worship of Canaan or Mesopotamia.[2]

Daniel smiled as he remembered how the priests and Levites used to fight among themselves, each trying to get power over the people. But now they had been forced to work together in harmony. The prophet's mind came back to the present as he neared the Chebar village. He came to a group of old men sitting cross-legged on the ground under a tree in front of the local inn.

"Ho, Daniel!" cried one of the men.

Daniel recognized the voice, and ran toward the man rising from the group. "Hananiah!" (Shadrach) he cried. The two locked each other in a warm embrace.

"I'm so glad you've come." Hananiah held Daniel at arms' length and looked deep into his eyes. He basked in the warmth of kinship they'd enjoyed together for so many years, but at last he spoke again. "Daniel, our people have become discouraged. Belshazzar's policies have made life difficult for them."

"I'm sorry to hear that." The joy that had shown in the old prophet's face melted into an expression of deep sadness.

"You'll remember that as chief buyer for palace supplies, I purchased a lot of grain and olive oil from our farmers and merchants," Hananiah explained. "But when the king's son replaced me with a Babylonian, our people lost their best market." The old man sighed. "I'm afraid some of them went out of business altogether."

"It does seem unfair," agreed Daniel.

"I visited most of the Jewish colonies in my work," Hananiah went on. "Our people had adopted the language and customs of the Babylonians. They owned lands and small businesses, and very few wanted to return to Judah."

"But that's all changed," remarked Daniel. "The hardships have caused them to think of home again—and that's good."

"It surely is." Hananiah chewed on a stalk of rye grass as he gazed downstream at a departing canal boat.

"Where have your two friends gone?" asked a man who had walked up and now stood beside them.

Hananiah's face wrinkled, and he scratched his head. "Azariah—Abednego . . ." He turned to Daniel. "Remember how much difficulty he experienced learning how to read and write the cuneiform script?"

Daniel laughed. "He thought he'd never understand all those 'hen scratches,' as he called them."

Turning back to the others, Hananiah went on. "Well, he served as the favorite scribe of Nebuchadnezzar's son, Amel-Marduk—from the prince's childhood until his brother-in-law murdered him. You know," he took the rye stalk out of his mouth and pointed it at Daniel, "I never thought about it before, but—I wonder if Azariah had anything to do with Amel-Marduk's releasing King Jehoiachin from prison?"

"No doubt about it," answered Daniel. "Nergal-shar-usur knew it too. That's why Azariah found a job in another city after Amel-Marduk died."

"Have you heard anything from Mishael [Meshach]?"

"He still works in the palace—last I heard," replied Daniel. "Nitocris told me once that she couldn't trust anyone but Mishael as steward of the royal harem."

"How'd he escape the wrath of Belshazzar?" asked an older woman.

"The son of the king tried to put him out," replied Daniel. "But Nitocris wouldn't let him." He smiled to himself and watched a group of slaves tugging at the ropes of an approaching barge. "I think she depends on him for advice as well."

The crowd laughed, pressing closer to the two elder statesmen. The experiences of these men in Babylon had made them the most popular Jews in the world, and everyone had questions to ask.

Children had joined the group as well, jumping up and

down around the men. "Tell us about the fiery furnace again, Hananiah," shouted a boy. "Were you scared?"

A girl elbowed her way to the front. "Was it hot in the furnace?" she asked, her eyes as large as shekel coins.

Other children shouted questions too, and the clamor became a bedlam.

"Hear! Hear! Quiet down!" demanded a village elder. "Daniel and Hananiah didn't come here to tell children's stories. Go home, you pesky urchins! Be off with you!"

A gentle hand touched the elder's shoulder, and he turned to look into Daniel's face. "Let's tell the children a story first," the prophet suggested. "Then they'll be happy, and we can talk in peace."

The elder shrugged and motioned for the children to sit down.

"Yes," began Hananiah when they had settled, "the furnace was hot. But no, it didn't burn us—and no, we weren't afraid . . ."

The children sat spellbound as Hananiah told them the story.

". . . And when we came out of the furnace," he concluded, "they didn't find a mark on us—not a hair singed—not even the smell of smoke.

"It reminded me of God's promise through Isaiah: 'When you pass through the waters, I will be with you; and when you pass through the rivers, they will not sweep over you. When you *walk through the fire*, you will *not be burned*; the *flames* will *not set you ablaze*. For I am the Lord, your God, the Holy One of Israel, your Savior.'[3]

"Nebuchadnezzar praised God too."

"Amen," chorused the people, as the children ran off to play.

"You've all been concerned by recent events in Babylon." Daniel looked over the small crowd. "It's a time that tries men's souls."

The people nodded.

The prophet outlined the instability of the past few years. "Jews everywhere thought Babylon would soon fall, and God would lead us home again.

"But now Nabonidus and Belshazzar have restored Babylon's power, and they're causing us more trouble than ever before."

"Isn't it time for the Messiah to come?" called a forlorn voice.

"Amen," shouted an elder. "Tell us, Daniel, when will He come and lead us back to Judah?"

Daniel studied the pebbles on the ground before speaking again. "Several months ago I had a dream that helped explain our future." He ran his fingers through his hair.

"In my vision at night I looked, and there before me were the four winds of heaven churning up the great sea. Four great beasts, each different from the others, came up out of the sea.

"The first was like a lion, and it had the wings of an eagle. I watched until its wings were torn off and it was lifted from the ground so that it stood on two feet like a man, and the heart of a man was given to it.

"And there before me was a second beast, which looked like a bear. It was raised up on one of its sides, and it had three ribs in its mouth. . . . It was told, 'Get up and eat your fill of flesh!'

"After that, I looked, and there before me was another beast, one that looked like a leopard. And on its back it had four wings like those of a bird. This beast had four heads, and it was given authority to rule.

"After that, . . . there before me was a fourth beast—terrifying and frightening and very powerful. It had large iron teeth; it crushed and devoured its victims and trampled underfoot whatever was left. It was different from all the former beasts, and it had ten horns. . . .

"As I looked, thrones were set in place, and the Ancient of Days took his seat. . . . Thousands upon thousands attended him; ten thousand times ten thousand stood before him. . . . I looked, and there before me was one like a son of man, coming with the clouds of heaven. He approached the Ancient of Days and . . . was given authority, glory and sovereign power; all peoples, nations and men of every language worshiped him.

His dominion is an everlasting dominion that will not pass away, and his kingdom is one that will never be destroyed."[4]

"That's the Messiah!" called a man who stood next to the tree. "He's coming soon to set up His kingdom."

Daniel nodded, but went on. "An angel said to me: 'The four great beasts are four kingdoms that will rise from the earth.'[5] The lion with eagle's wings must be Babylon, for that's the symbol she uses for herself."

"The wings were plucked off, and a man's heart was given to it," chimed in a Levite sitting near the front. "That must mean that the empire will become weak."

"That's right." Daniel grinned. "We're living in that time right now."

"But your dream doesn't show the Messiah coming now." The priest's deeply creased forehead showed his concern.

"No," Daniel replied. "The Messiah will come at some future time. However, Babylon *is* nearing its end. God will soon open the gates so we can go home—and that's good news!"

★　　　　★　　　　★　　　　★

While Nabonidus occupied himself with the Arabs, and Belshazzar amassed his personal fortune at the expense of virtually everyone, Nitocris used her talents in more constructive ways. As a child, she'd always wondered at her father's great building projects. She'd observed his contractors build great temples, walls, and gates, and had developed a remarkable degree of engineering skill merely through watching them.

When Nebuchadnezzar died, Nitocris mourned the loss of her father. She also grieved for his unfinished projects. "If only he could have completed them all," she wailed to her husband after the funeral. "Then he'd have worthy monuments to remind future generations of his greatness."

"He's already built more than a hundred kings before him," consoled Nabonidus. "No one will ever forget him."

"I know," she whimpered. "It's just that . . ."

"That you enjoyed watching his buildings grow," chided her husband. "You'd have given up your royal ancestry just to have a part in the design and construction yourself."

"You noticed?" She dried her eyes and gazed at her husband. "I know it's not a woman's position, but . . ."

"Never mind, Nitocris." He enfolded her with his massive arms and touched his forehead to hers. "Perhaps someday you can finish your father's work."

It had seemed an impossible dream to the wife of a court official, but when Nabonidus rose to power, the old instincts returned. So when her husband went on his extended military missions, Nitocris resurrected her father's old blueprints and hired builders to begin work.

"My father built the suburban housing district across the river," she told one contractor, "and he never built a bridge to connect it with the old city."

"We'll need money and materials—and many laborers," returned the builder.

"You shall have them," she replied, a feeling of euphoria passing over her. "I'm in contact with the king almost daily through the royal messenger service. If any matters arise beyond my authority, I can have his reply within a week or two."

During Nabonidus's absence she completed the bridge— resting it upon imported stone piers—and beautified many temples. She also altered the course of the Euphrates River above Babylon so that any invader would have difficulty attacking from that direction. She dug a large reservoir north of the city to store rainy-season runoff water to use in filling irrigation canals during dry months.

"Father would be proud that I've finished his projects," she told Belshazzar. "I only wish you could become as great a king as he."

"I *am* great," growled her son. "If you'd stop interfering with my decisions, I'd be even greater."

"Your decisions are often faulty, my son."

"Faulty!" he roared. "What do you mean, 'faulty'?"

"Your heart has become perverse." A tear formed in the corner of her eye, and she leaned forward, placing her hand on his. "Your father failed to discipline you when you were younger. You always got your way whether it was good or bad, and now you have a flawed character. I fear that only the God of Daniel and Nebuchadnezzar can change you."

"Don't speak to me about Him!" shouted Belshazzar, jerking his hand away from hers. "I hate Him—and Daniel—and all his kind! I'll never bow to the God of the Jews!"

"Then you can never be great, my son," she wailed, burying her face in her hands. "Someday you'll fall. And when you do, all my work—and my father's before me—and all Babylon—will fall into alien hands."

---

1. Actual text of a clay tablet showing a business transaction made for Belshazzar.
2. Leviticus 23:10-13; 18:1-5.
3. See Isaiah 43:2, 3, emphasis supplied.
4. Daniel 7:2-14.
5. Daniel 7:17.

Chapter 3

Rise of the Eastern Star

"Is your master well?" asked the king of Anshan.

The ambassador bowed before Cyrus. "The great king, King Nabonidus of Babylon—yes, my lord, the king is well." The Babylonian had difficulty breathing in the thin air of the high Persian plateau and had not yet recovered from the rigorous trek over tortuous mountain trails.

"I'm pleased he's well," returned Cyrus, "and gratified he sent you to discuss terms of peace."

Cyrus had done well for himself. He grew up as a member of the Achaemenidae family, son of Cambyses I and Mandane, who was daughter of the Median King Astyages. His ancestors had ruled the Pasargadae tribe for generations, but he'd spent much of his childhood hiding from the murderous plots of those who wanted to take over the throne.

More than a match for his enemies, Cyrus became king in spite of their efforts to kill him. He soon gained the support of two neighboring tribes—the Maraphii and the Maspii—and before long secured the allegiance of all the Persian tribes. Now he had become greater than any Achaemenidaen king before him.

Persia lay under the control of the powerful Median kingdom to its northwest, ruled now by Cyrus's wealthy and corrupt grandfather, King Astyages. This ruler had opposed his grandson at first, for he realized that the young man's personal power could threaten the Median throne.

The Persian people, however, insisted that the young man become their ruler, so at last Astyages granted Cyrus the position of vassal king. The Mede sought to prevent trouble by placing restrictions on his powers. He also planted spies in the palace at Pasargadae, but Cyrus uncovered them and reassigned them so they'd have to depend upon loyal Persians for their information.

When the Babylonian envoy came, Cyrus was grateful that none of the spies could hear his voice. His own men would give them a report, but their information would conceal the real purpose of the visit.

"As my envoys told your master," Cyrus continued, carefully wording his proposition, "I want to form an alliance with Babylon."

"Do all that you have in mind," returned the ambassador. The polite phrase meant that he was willing to listen to the proposal.

"There has been friction between Babylon and Media," Cyrus went on. He leaned forward and spoke softly so his voice wouldn't carry to any rooms nearby. "Media wants to seat their king on Babylon's throne."

"My lord has good information." The envoy's eyes bulged as he realized that the "secret" feud had become public knowledge.

During the reign of Nabopolassar, Babylon and Media had become allies in order to destroy Assyria. But undercurrents of hostility strained their alliance almost to the breaking point.

Babylon's military power had decayed during the reigns of the weak kings who followed Nebuchadnezzar. Now Nabonidus sought desperately to strengthen it, but Media posed a real threat. The Babylonian king didn't feel prepared to fight a major rival yet and needed a few more years to consolidate his forces.

Cyrus looked both ways, assuring himself that no spies could hear him. "I also have a disagreement with Media," he whispered, "and I believe we can help each other."

"Say on," replied the envoy.

"Nabonidus wants time to build and train his armies," Cyrus suggested, "and I can buy him the time he needs." The Persian rose from his throne, descended the steps, and stopped beside the envoy. "If Nabonidus will occupy his armies in the Westland, I'll keep Media off his back."

"We still have a treaty with Media," returned the ambassador, scratching the side of his head. "They'll surely ask for help if your armies get the upper hand."

"Yes," answered Cyrus, hands on his hips. "But you'll find some excuse why you cannot help them. I can defeat Media, but not the combined armies of Media and Babylon."

The ambassador nodded his head. "It sounds reasonable. I can't see why the great king, King Nabonidus of Babylon, wouldn't agree to that." He mentally reviewed the objectives he'd discussed before his journey and decided that Cyrus's strategy meshed well with Nabonidus's plans. "Yes," he concluded. "King Nabonidus will agree to that."

Cyrus bowed in the temple of his god, offering the sacrifices required by the priests. He had a broad mind and believed that by respecting all the gods, he would have unlimited blessings. Like most Aryan people, he adored a set of nature-gods, but he also recognized a Supreme Being to whom the Persians had given many names. To this Supreme God, Cyrus now paid his humble respects. He expected in return to receive a blessing and strength to conquer his enemies.

Leaving the temple, Cyrus mounted his horse and joined his royal guards. Though watchful of danger, they relaxed as they rode into the hills beyond the edges of the wall-less capital city. The young king enjoyed the clear air and the magnificent views. One after another, succeeding mountain ranges extended beyond the nearby slopes all the way to the horizon.

The group hadn't gone far when a palace courier galloped up and read Cyrus a message.

"What?" he shouted, his face turning crimson. "Astyages did what?"

The king hadn't bothered to stop when the page approached, but now he reigned up his horse abruptly. The mounted guards surrounding him bumped into each other in their attempts to avoid colliding with their king. One of them toppled from his steed and rolled down a steep embankment. He sprang to his feet grinning, brushed himself off, and scrambled back up the incline.

"He executed the son of General Harpagus," replied the page calmly. Though messengers of other ancient kings feared to bring bad news—angry monarchs sometimes killed heralds—Cyrus treated his servants with justice.

The intensity of Cyrus's fury made it impossible for him to speak. All the pleasure he'd known only minutes before evaporated at the news of another Astyagean atrocity, and he spurred his mount back toward the palace.

"Grandfather's a tyrant!" he shouted as he exploded into his bedroom. He tossed his riding clothes in all directions as he removed them. The king's valet jogged after him, picking up the clothes and trying to make sense of his rambling words.

"Astyages, the 'lance-hurler'!" The king spat out the name. "There he sits, surrounded with luxury, filling his days with feasting and drinking and every sort of pleasure while his people rot in poverty." He kicked over a table beside his bed. "He's been on that throne for thirty-five years—and it all comes down to this!"

Cyrus paced back and forth in the room, striding with quick, stomping steps, gesturing with his fist. "Of all things!" he shouted. He still couldn't believe the news. "He killed the son of his leading general for petty thievery! He'd have only flogged a common beggar for that. Who does he think he is—God?"

It seemed to Cyrus that someone had tied his stomach into knots. His heart galloped at full tilt, and he had difficulty breathing. He'd never before felt such loathing toward anyone like he felt just now toward his Median master. "Where's that messenger?" he barked. "I've got to know exactly what happened."

The page's story remained unchanged. He'd gotten every

detail of the sad affair from the general himself while he mourned for his son.

"Grandfather!" Cyrus's face contorted at the thought of the old Median king. "You didn't succeed in killing me, but you got Harpagus's son. Someone has to put an end to your oppression." He continued his circuit around the room. "We've got to give the people a chance to live without fear."

The king stopped for several minutes, stroking his beard and gazing out the window at the distant mountains. After what seemed like hours to the page, Cyrus made his decision. Turning to a scribe who sat on a bench nearby, he issued an order.

"Call up a general conscription," he commanded. "I want every able-bodied man to come to Pasargadae prepared for war. I'm going to put an end to the tyranny of Astyages—once and for all."

★   ★   ★   ★

Word of the military buildup reached Astyages with the speed of his spy network.

"Cyrus? Raising an army?" The obese monarch took a handful of grapes and wolfed them down, seeds and all, while he listened to his intelligence officer. He grinned as juice dribbled from the corners of his mouth and stained his graying beard. "Whatever for?" He laughed. "Having trouble with his warlike neighbors again?"

"No, my lord," returned the officer, disgusted with the king's filthy manners and his refusal to take the threat seriously. "He plans to march on Media."

"Delusions of grandeur," chuckled Astyages. "The rare mountain air has fogged his brain. He hasn't a chance against my troopers, and he knows it." The king guzzled a full goblet of wine without so much as a breath of air and handed it to his chamberlain for a refill. "How long do you think he'll need to raise an army?"

"Many soldiers have already gathered in Pasargadae," answered the spy chief. "He talks like he'll be ready to march within the month."

"That rabble he calls an army will need a lot of training before they'll be ready for my men." The Median king belched, and smiled. Visions of beggars, cripples, tenant farmers, and old tradesmen trying to learn how to use weapons of war danced in his intoxicated head. "Even if he succeeds in training them to fight, I doubt he'll find enough wagons to transport their supplies across the mountains."

"May the king live forever," the officer bowed, "but my lord's knowledge of the Persians is incomplete." He hesitated to give a negative report for fear he might be executed. "The soldiers I saw in Pasargadae were young and strong and already well-trained. My lord needs to move quickly before Cyrus completes his plans."

"Since when did you become my advisor?!" thundered Astyages. He lunged from the throne and struck the spy chief across the face, knocking him to the ground. "I could have your head for such insolence!"

Cooling quickly, the Median monarch returned to the royal chair, breathing heavily from the exertion. His terrified victim cowered on the floor, expecting the palace guard to haul him off for execution. "Nevertheless," the king smiled as if nothing had happened, "you've done fine work." He reached for another fistful of grapes. "Now go back to Persia and keep me informed."

Astyages giggled as the pale officer slunk from the room, wishing he'd never entered the royal service.

"Page!" barked the king. "Send for General Harpagus. I have a little job for him."

★   ★   ★   ★

"What do you know about Cyrus?" General Harpagus guided his black stallion along the narrow mountain trail, his army stretching before and behind him for miles.

The general's advisor licked his lips and deliberated before speaking. "My cousin lives in Pasargadae." He scanned the ridge above them for possible enemy scouts. "Came to see us a few months ago. Told how people in Persia are happy, well-fed, have plenty of work."

"Sounds good," returned Harpagus. "Did he speak of Cyrus?"

"Yes," The advisor grasped for words to express what he'd heard. "People love him. Quick to punish offenders and to reward good service."

The two rode on for several minutes as the general conferred with a messenger. "The forward platoons are nearly at the summit, my lord," related the courier. "Advance scouts indicate no hostile forces in sight."

"We have to cross two more mountain ranges before we reach enemy territory," returned the general. "Tell my scouts to be careful. Cyrus might have posted lookouts or advanced guards in these mountains."

"Yes, my lord," replied the page as he spurred his mount toward the head of the column. He used care not to slip off the narrow trail into the canyon far below.

"I don't like these twisting mountain trails," complained Harpagus. "Our soldiers march in a long, thin line for miles. If Cyrus surprised us in just the right place . . ." He glanced along the queue as it snaked its way up the winding path from the valley far below. He drew his breath in, making a whistle. "He could destroy us with only a few commando units!"

"He's capable of that, my lord," returned the advisor.

"Oh?" The general stared at his friend.

"My cousin said Cyrus has unique talents for leading men." He uncorked his goatskin canteen and sipped a mouthful of water. "Fights with them. They're loyal to all his commands."

"That's no different from any other good commander," argued the general. He felt jealous that his trusted friend showed partiality to a man he'd never met!

"Yes—and no." The advisor turned in his saddle so he could face his chief. "I've served you well. My life is in your hands. You're my master, my friend." He wrinkled his forehead. "I've fought at your side in battles large and small. Laughed with you. Wept with you." He deliberately omitted mentioning the death of Harpagus's son.

"I've never knowingly given you false counsel," he continued, glancing at the road ahead to confirm that his horse maintained its place in line. Staring into the distance for several minutes, his eyes traced the lines of the misty mountains, range upon range. They resembled ranks of dominoes as far as the eye could see.

"What are you getting at?" Harpagus's patience wore a thin shell.

"This." The advisor paused again, searching for a way to express his feelings. "My words may sound treasonous, but they come from the heart. Destroying Cyrus will not benefit our people."

"What?" The general couldn't believe what he'd heard.

The counselor lowered his voice. "Cyrus seems a better king—a better man than any monarch I've known." He didn't openly name the Median king they'd served during the past thirty-five years.

"You mean—" Harpagus stopped. He had longed for a more humane ruler, but had feared to express such thoughts. His grief and anger over the way Astyages executed his son had failed to heal with time. Instead, his feelings toward his master had festered into an inner contempt for the king and all his policies.

The counselor held up his hand for silence. He knew the general understood him, but he didn't want his chief to voice opinions for which he would be required to answer.

The two rode on without speaking, their hearts filled with turmoil. To proceed according to their desires would be deemed treason, punishable by death—if caught. But to carry out Astyages's orders to crush Cyrus was unthinkable.

Just thinking about disobedience to their king cut directly across the web of both their characters. They'd loyally served the Median throne all their lives. Never, in thought or word or action, could anyone accuse them of working against the best interests of Astyages. Even the idea of treason filled Harpagus with disgust.

Then a mental image of his son floated up before him. The lad had been his lifelong joy, his hope for the future. He'd been loyal to his family, hard-working, gentle, manly—how could Astyages do such a thing? How could he execu—? The memory pierced his heart, starting the emotional hemorrhage all over again. Tears filled his eyes. He fought to control them, hoping his men hadn't seen.

"Let them flow," his counselor advised him, placing a hand on the general's shoulder. "Get it out of your system. The child is gone. We can't bring him back. It's all right to grieve."

The general pondered a new option. He could break away from Media. He could unite with the "righteous" king of Persia and serve a master who had a heart. He could fight against Astyages and revenge the death of his son. He could . . . No, it all seemed too radical to his loyal mind.

The two men topped the mountain crest and scanned the twisting column of marching men on the descending trails ahead. They marveled at the range after range of jagged peaks that marched toward the horizon. The clear, thin air foreshortened the scene, causing the faraway mountains to appear close at hand. As the succeeding ranges paraded into the distance, they faded into shades of purple, until they disappeared from view under the curvature of the earth.

Harpagus glanced back at the following army still tramping up the steep grade. His heart wept for these poor, misused souls who'd been under Astyages's heel all their lives. What a pity! he thought. Now they go to face one of the great generals of our time. Many will die—and for what? So their families can continue to live as miserably as before?

The general dabbed at a tear that trickled from the corner of his eye. There's no justice in it, he thought. Someone has to rescue them, give them something to live for, something to fight for; give their families hope for the future. His mind warred against itself. He tried to balance his fidelity to a monarch he'd pledged to serve for a lifetime with his love for these men and their families.

A sword whipped through his mind, hacking away at his fanatical loyalty to Astyages. The murderous blade dripped with blood—the blood of his own son. He peered at the countenance of the sneering warrior who brandished the weapon, and his face was the face of—Astyages!

"Look." His counselor-companion pointed down the forward

slope, interrupting his superior's mental turmoil. "A rider. Passing our troops up the trail."

"One of my messengers," returned Harpagus without emotion. "Perhaps he has some word from our scouts."

As the page approached, Harpagus gathered from his haste that he carried a crucial message. Perhaps his advance units had already engaged the enemy.

"My lord." The page nodded his head in the merest reflection of a bow. "I have a communiqué for you from Cyrus, king of Persia."

Cyrus! wondered the general. Why would Cyrus send me a message? Does he fear the might of Astyages? The power of Harpagus?

The messenger handed the general a scroll, and the military man passed it on to his counselor—a trained scribe.

"Peace and goodwill to Harpagus, general of the armies of Media," the letter began.

Strange, thought Harpagus, that my enemy would address me in such friendly terms. He wrestled to control his chaotic thoughts so he could concentrate on the message.

The counselor continued to read: "I extend to you my warmest sympathies on the death of your beloved firstborn son. My heart breaks at the injustice done to you and your family."

Giant waves of grief broke over Harpagus, drowning out his senses, and he waved his counselor silent. He hadn't heard such kindness from anyone—not even his dearest friends. They had all feared to mourn with him, lest the angry Astyages butcher their beloved as well. The general grappled with his emotions for many minutes before he regained control of them.

"I do not wish to fight you and inflict more grief upon the homes of Media," the message went on. "Come to Pasargadae as my guest. Let us mourn your loss together. We will care for your needs and send you home to your master rejoicing."

Harpagus couldn't believe his ears. Once he would have considered such a communiqué a mere mockery, sent to incite anger and fighting. But the tone of the message matched everything he knew about Cyrus. It touched his heart.

"What a man!" he remarked. "What a contrast to the spirit of the one we've served so long."

"How true." The counselor smiled. He too had seen the sender's sincerity and felt drawn to know more about this man Cyrus.

"I can't fight a man like this." The general clenched his fist. "I can't destroy a leader who understands the yearning of men's hearts and judges without guile."

The horses began the descent, following the trail without human guidance. Median troops, before and behind, continued their trek, unaware of the momentous alternatives awash within their leader's heart—choices that would alter and brighten their entire future.

"Page!" called the general. "Take a message for Cyrus."

The herald had withdrawn to follow several yards behind his leader. Now he urged his mount to Harpagus's side, removed his writing materials from their pouch, and prepared to inscribe the message.

"Cyrus, king of Anshan. Greetings." The general contemplated what he'd say, wanting to choose the right words for this, the most important letter of his life. "I accept your sympathy for my dead son and your invitation to mourn with me. I request safe conduct for myself and my bodyguard. We will come to you in peace."

★   ★   ★   ★

"Astyages has gathered a large army, my lord." The herald interrupted the noon meal of Cyrus, Harpagus, and their officers. "He leads them in person."

Cyrus smiled. He'd hoped for an opportunity like this, for he believed the ease-loving king would panic when warfare broke out around him. "Can you imagine his Magnificence actually traveling over those rugged mountain trails?" he asked his companions.

Harpagus laughed. "He may not survive long enough to fight you, my lord. I only wish I were there to enjoy his misery." By now the Median general had pledged his loyalty to the Persian king, joining his immense army with that of

Cyrus. Now an angry Astyages came to punish him for his "treason."

"What will be our chances against his army when they arrive?" Cyrus broke off a morsel of bread and ate it after dipping it into a goblet of wine.

"If we fight," replied Harpagus, "he won't stand a chance. I've brought all the veteran soldiers over to your side. He has nothing but raw recruits. Some may show great zeal, wanting to impress His Highness, but the battle will surely be ours."

"Can we win without a fight?" Cyrus knew Harpagus might misunderstand. The Persian had no hesitancy in fighting the Median army, but he often sought ways to prevent the bloodshed and grief that accompanied every war. "Can we persuade his soldiers to lay down their weapons, to quit before the battle starts?"

"That would be gratifying, wouldn't it?" Harpagus smiled at the flash of imagery flitting across his mind: Astyages shouting "Charge!" but his troops laying down their weapons and refusing to fight.

During the next few days, while Harpagus and his generals prepared to do battle with their brothers, Cyrus recruited Median soldiers for another purpose. He trained them and sent them alone and in small groups—on different routes—to join Astyages's army. Their mission: to undermine the morale of the rank and file, and to destroy their faith in their king.

When the Median army marched into sight of the Persian's wall-less capital, Cyrus searched the multitude for a sign of its commander in chief. Near the rear, he spied an ornate chariot and recognized his grandfather's face. Astyages had made it over the mountains, but the haggard old man appeared so tired he could hardly stand.

While Cyrus watched, he saw the aged king muster what little strength he had left to shout orders to his men. The words drifted out over the restless armies and reached the Persian's ears.

"Attack the rebels!" he screamed. "Show no mercy! Take Cyrus and Harpagus alive!" He began to cough uncontrollably from the strain. His lieutenant gave him a goblet of wine, which he upended, and soon had himself under control again. "I want to punish those two," he bellowed. "I want to see them suffer for the trouble they've caused me. I want . . ."

"Who is Astyages?" cried a Median soldier, near the king's chariot. "We want Cyrus!"

"Seize him!" shouted Astyages. "Slay him here before me!"

The man refused to be quiet. "We want Cyrus!" he sang, and others joined him. Within seconds, the entire Median army chanted together: "We want Cyrus! We want Cyrus!"

The earth shuddered with the roar, and Cyrus grinned. His own Persians and Harpagus's Medes joined in the chant until tens of thousands of voices echoed the joyous call: "We want Cyrus! We want Cyrus!"

Astyages flew into a rage, drew his sword, and began hacking away at those who stood near him. Several hapless fellows fell before the king's own bodyguard disarmed him. They bound the old man and led him through the mob toward the city's entrance, where Cyrus stood.

Without command, the two armies rushed at each other, but not a weapon could be seen. Instead, the men charged headlong—arms open wide—joyfully welcoming their brothers into the service of Cyrus. The men who held Astyages found themselves surrounded by so many well-wishers that for a time they feared they might be crushed by the throng.

The joy became so infectious that seasoned soldiers threw down their weapons, grasped anyone nearby, and danced for joy. The chant changed and became a shout of triumph—melting into an oath of allegiance: "Long live Cyrus! Long live Cyrus!"

A group of Persian soldiers emerged from the city carrying Cyrus on their shoulders. They deposited him on a watchtower where all could see him. And the frolic went on for hours. The Medes had come to fight and die for a tyrant they all hated. Instead they'd deposed Astyages and replaced him with Cyrus—a man of love and justice whom all could serve with honor.

★   ★   ★   ★

Astyages faced justice at last in Pasargadae. During his trial so many witnesses produced their testimony that even the wicked king himself began to realize how far he had fallen. He accepted the sentence of death without murmur.

Word of Astyages's execution swept through Persia and Media with amazing speed. People rejoiced and praised the wisdom and justice of their new king—Cyrus the Persian.

Cyrus granted Media full freedom and made it the first satrapy (state) of Persia—called "Mada." The inhabitants felt magnanimous toward him and called him "king of the Medes," a title of honor. Persians and Medes became equals and worked together for the benefit of the empire. Cyrus removed all the palace treasures from Ecbatana and transported them to Anshan. But for years to come, Persian kings enjoyed sojourning at the beautiful palace of Astyages.

Chapter 4

One Last Chance

"Where is the Jewish colony in Susa?" asked Daniel as he came near a man who worked beside the road.

Daniel approached Susa, the capital of Elam, its citadel rising high over the Ulai Canal. The fort's harsh lines reflected from the 900-foot-wide man-made waterway, and Daniel drank in the beauty of the scene. The sun had passed midheaven by now. Temperatures soared to an uncomfortable level, and the old man wanted to find some shade.

The working man didn't answer or even notice that Daniel had asked him a question. So the prophet touched his shoulder. "Where is the Jewish colony in Susa?" he asked again.

The worker pointed to his mouth and his ear, and Daniel realized that the man could neither speak nor hear. So Daniel pointed to his own beardless face, and gestured with his hands to show that he sought men who wore a distinctive style of beard.

The deaf man smiled and nodded, pointing down the road. After many gestures, he made Daniel understand that he would find some Jews if he turned right at the next crossroad.

Daniel grinned, patted the deaf man on the shoulder, and placed a shekel coin in his hand. As the prophet strode toward the city, the worker watched him and marveled at his kindness.

Turning right at the corner, Daniel spied a group of men sitting under an overspreading tree. As he approached, he recognized them as a collection of Jews who had gathered here to rest in the afternoon heat. Nearing the human cluster, he observed their long faces and guessed that they all suffered from discouragement.

Daniel sat down with the assembly and tried to encourage them. Many felt homesick for Judah. Even those who had been born in Babylon longed for the day when they could return to the land of their ancestors.

"If only we could go home," bemoaned a young man. "Then we could worship at the temple—just like our fathers did."

"But the Babylonians destroyed the temple," reminded Daniel.

"I know." The unhappy youth studied his sandals for a time and then looked back at Daniel. "But we'll rebuild it, we will. Just you wait and see."

Daniel smiled at the young man's zeal and patted his knee. "Yes, my son, we'll rebuild it. But all in God's good time."

The prophet brought them greetings from Jews in other colonies and related his vision of the four great beasts coming up out of the sea. The people became excited when they realized that God still cared for them. Soon Babylon would fall, and they could go back to Judah. Best of all, Daniel assured them that one day, Messiah would come and set all things right again.

The sun set behind the citadel before they broke up and went to their homes. One of the elders invited Daniel to spend the night with him, and the prophet agreed.

During the night, the seer had another dream.

"I looked up," he told the people on the following day, "and there before me was a ram with two horns, standing beside the canal, and the horns were long. One of the horns was longer than the other but grew up later. I watched the ram as he charged toward the west and the north and the south. No animal could stand against him, and none could rescue from his power. He did as he pleased and became great.

"As I was thinking about this, suddenly a goat with a prominent horn between his eyes came from the west, crossing the whole earth without touching the ground. He came toward the two-horned ram I had seen standing beside the canal and charged at him with great rage. I saw him attack the ram furiously, striking the ram and shattering his two horns. The ram was powerless to stand against him; the goat knocked him to the ground and trampled on him, and none could rescue the ram from his power."[1]

"An angel came to me again, and explained the vision. He said: 'The two-horned ram that you saw represents the kings of Media and Persia. The shaggy goat is the king of Greece, and the large horn between his eyes is the first king.' "[2]

"That's a strange dream," said one of the women standing near the back of the crowd. "Media is a strong empire, we all know that. But what is Persia?"

"It's just a little mountain province far to the south and east," explained Daniel.

"That's right," agreed a scribe who sat in the front row. "They have a king named Cyrus, a nephew of General Gobryas, I believe." He scratched his head and looked around, feeling very important. "I heard in the marketplace just this morning that Cyrus has rebelled against the Medes. King Astyages has sent a large army to Persia to put down the revolt."

Several people spoke at once, expressing their surprise at this news.

"But, Daniel." The scribe looked concerned. "You didn't see anything in this vision about Babylon."

"No," replied Daniel. "It seems that Media and Persia will conquer Babylon." He paused for a moment to consider what he'd just said. "Yes," he thought aloud. "The angel said Media and Persia could move in any direction, for no nation could stand against them. So Babylon will fall to the Medes and the Persians sometime before the events of this dream take place." He looked into the distance for a moment. "Knowing this, I think we could safely say that the bear I saw in the other vision represents those two countries as well."

Daniel licked his lips before speaking again. "These visions teach us some important lessons. First, Babylon will come to an end, and another nation will replace it. The conqueror will then allow God's people to return to Judah.

"Another lesson I've learned is that God is in control. All the play and counterplay of forces we see around us fit into His larger plan to save all mankind from their sins.

"We all want to return to Jerusalem and rebuild the temple, don't we?"

A chorus of "Amens" drifted up from the crowd.

"The third lesson I've learned explains the spiritual work we must do before we'll be ready to go." Daniel studied the faces of his audience to see if they understood what he said. "We must return to God with all our hearts," he continued. "We must learn to obey His laws. We must allow God's Spirit to mold our thoughts and actions so they'll be in harmony with His Word."

"But how can we do that?" asked a young man who sat cross-legged on the ground.

"We need to spend much time in studying the Scriptures and in praying," answered Daniel.

"How can we pray?" asked another man, shifting his legs to another position to allow proper circulation.

"When you pray," Daniel returned, "give thanks to God for all He's done for you. Don't tell Him your problems first, because that will only make them seem larger, and it might cause your faith to falter.

"Instead, quote to God some of the promises you've found in the holy writings, and say to Him, 'I believe You.' Think of all His blessings and give thanks for them too. After you've done this, then tell Him your difficulties.

"When you pray like this, your faith will be stronger, and your problems will seem smaller. Never entertain any doubts—not even for a moment. God hears every prayer of faith, and He'll answer you when He feels the right time has come.

"Remember when Solomon consecrated the temple?" Daniel

went on. Heads nodded all around. "He told us what to do when we find ourselves in captivity. Listen to what he said in his prayer of dedication." The parchment scroll in Daniel's hands crinkled as he unrolled it to the place he'd selected.

" 'When they sin against you [God]—for there is no one who does not sin—and you become angry with them and give them over to the enemy, who takes them captive to his own land, far away or near; and if they have a change of heart in the land where they are held captive, and repent and plead with you in the land of their conquerors and say, "We have sinned, we have done wrong, we have acted wickedly"; and if they turn back to you with all their heart and soul . . . and pray to you toward the land you gave their fathers, toward the city you have chosen and the temple I have built for your Name; then from heaven, your dwelling place, hear their prayer and their plea, and uphold their cause. And forgive your people, who have sinned against you; forgive all the offenses they have committed against you, and cause their conquerors to show them mercy.'[3]

"Be of good cheer," Daniel continued. "Spend much time in prayer and in studying the law and the prophets. Prepare your hearts. Then, when God's time comes, you'll be ready to return to Judah.

"Soon God will send a deliverer," he promised. "Soon He'll open the gates of Babylon and permit His people to go free."

★   ★   ★   ★

"So, Astyages fell to Cyrus." Croesus, king of Lydia, basked in the sunlight on the roof of his castle-palace. For the thousandth time, he felt awed by the beauty of the broad Hermus valley and by the precipitous cliffs upon which he'd built his capital city. Because of Croesus' wealth and fame, Sardis had become world famous as a center of arts and letters.

"Astyages, ha!" laughed Croesus. "That old bag of wind has caused me trouble for years. I'm pleased that someone finally popped his bubble."

"Someone from far to the east," agreed the king's companion, "who'll likely have no dreams of conquest this far west."

"Don't count on it," countered the king. "I hear that Cyrus is an energetic, ambitious man."

"When he conquered Media," put in a military attaché who stood nearby, "he gained one of the best armies in the world."

Croesus shot an angry glance at the general. "*No* army is better than mine!" he declared. "Not even Media won against Lydia's finest troops."

Croesus not only had a valiant army, but many considered him one of the richest men on earth. He'd gotten his wealth from his mining operations and from gold dust his men had extracted from the Pactolus, a river flowing by the base of his citadel. Through the years, he'd developed the Lydian kingdom into a strong nation and enlarged its boundaries to include most of Asia Minor (modern Turkey).

Several years ago, he'd made an alliance with Babylon. A young court official, Nabonidus, represented Nebuchadnezzar and brought about peace between Lydia and Media. Croesus liked the Babylonian and felt he'd make a fine diplomat.

Now, Nabonidus had become king in Babylon, and Croesus had been disappointed. The Babylonian hadn't lived up to the Lydian's expectations.

"Nabonidus wants to renew his compact with me." Croesus eyed his chamberlain, who sat on a bench nearby. "Has his envoy given you any details?"

"Yes," replied the ancient man. He ran his gnarled fingers over his bald head and wished he'd worn a hat to protect it from the sun. "I don't see any difference between this and the one you made several years ago."

"Except that Nabonidus wants us to protect each other against Cyrus, should he attack either of our nations."

"Precisely," returned the chamberlain. "Cyrus just crossed the Tigris River and has captured Arbela and Haran. I'm sure that has something to do with the urgency of his current appeal. . . . Oh, yes, and Nabonidus wants to include Egypt in this alliance."

Croesus sighed. "Do I need to see the ambassador again?"

"Not if you agree to the terms of the treaty."

"Good." Croesus rose and strolled toward the stairs leading to the palace. "Let's go below. I have a proposal to make."

The elite group gathered in a small room. The king bent over a table on which he'd spread a map of Lydia and another of Media. "I've had my eye on this part of Cappadocia for a long time." He pointed to an area within the horseshoe bend of the Halys River. "With Astyages gone, we should have little difficulty taking it."

"Cyrus claims to control all the area that once belonged to Media," objected the chamberlain. "He might declare war on us if we stick our noses into his territory."

"I hear he's a real fighter," cautioned the general. "I think we can take him, you understand, but . . ." He put his finger to his lips, hesitating to speak his mind. "I wonder if that area is worth all the bloodshed, should Cyrus challenge us."

"Don't worry about Cyrus," scoffed Croesus. "We've joined with Babylon and Egypt. Cyrus is too wise to risk warfare with an alliance this size."

The king swatted a fly that had landed on the map. "Besides." His grin widened. "He'll have his hands full organizing Media's government. He'll have to police the whole country with his little band of Persian soldiers. He can't afford to invade a small province like Cappadocia before he consolidates his new holdings."

"Croesus has made a major miscalculation." Cyrus smiled. "He thinks I'm bogged down with occupying Media." The king of Persia and his chamberlain watched the last of Ecbatana's treasures begin their journey to Pasargadae. This wealth will support my plan to overthrow Babylon and form an empire of my own, the Persian thought. Then people everywhere will have peace and justice.

"He doesn't realize," returned the official cupbearer, "that the Medians accepted you gladly. They've pledged full support to your cause."

Cyrus marshaled the combined armies of Media and Persia, preparing to attack the Lydian aggressor in the west. As he reviewed the troops, he boasted to a general who stood nearby. "We have the largest army in history. No one can defeat us."

The grand war machine surged forward, climbing upward over the twisting trails west of Ecbatana. The chill winds blew, and isolated patches of snow melted in the late spring sunlight. As they passed through the gap at the top of the ridge, the view took their breath away. Several smaller ridges crossed their path, descending at last onto the distant Mesopotamian plains.

The road wound down the mountainside until it reached the Zagros Mountains at the "Gate of Asia." Beyond the "Gate," the trail descended even more rapidly. The cold air became warmer, and the foliage changed. Poplars, cypresses, and plane trees of the high plateau gave way to occasional palms. The army had reached the Mesopotamian prairie.

Rather than turn southward to assault Babylon—his final goal—Cyrus turned north toward Arbela in Assyria. Media had conquered Assyria several decades before, and Astyages had ruled the country with an iron hand. Happy to be free from the tyranny of the old king, the people of Arbela greeted Cyrus with joy, offering to help him in his wars. In return, Cyrus made Arbela the capital of the new province.

The Media-Persian army crossed the Tigris River below Arbela and headed north again. The citizens of Asshur resisted Cyrus for a time, but the city soon fell. Just before the fall, though, some of the zealous priests escaped with the city's god and carried the idol to Babylon for safekeeping. Without waiting for Cyrus's arrival, the priests of Nineveh did the same.

Passing on through Syria and Haran, Cyrus and his army followed the Great Road into Cilicia. The populace living in this area had been independent for generations, long known as wise people. When the monstrous army approached, they decided to accept Cyrus as their overlord, with only one condition: They wanted to keep their own native kings. Cyrus agreed.

Farther west, Cyrus passed through the Cilician Gates and organized Cappadocia into a new satrapy—Katpatuka. He also set up Armenia as the satrapy of Armina.

He now stood face to face with Croesus, the first serious opposition his force had met. The two armies clashed at Pteria and fought ferociously, leaving many thousands dead and dying on both sides. Neither army won a decisive victory, and Croesus withdrew his battered regiments to Sardis.

Safely inside his castle, Croesus felt relieved. "No enemy can break into my citadel," he boasted, falling into a nearby chair. "It doesn't matter how many men they have, they could never climb the walls or scale the cliffs."

On the next day, he rode his horse along the lines of surviving soldiers, encouraging them as best he could. "You're safe," he consoled. "Cyrus and his hordes can't hurt you here."

Croesus had miscalculated again. While Cyrus's main force made a show of preparing to attack from the front, trained mountain men studied the cliffs and mapped their route up its sheer face. On the fourteenth day of the siege, the mountain climbers scaled the acropolis, entered the city, and opened the main gates.

As Persian commandos fought hand to hand in the streets, and Cyrus's hordes poured through the main gates, Croesus lost his self-assurance. He knew that Eastern kings often executed conquered leaders—after putting them through gruesome torture.

So as Media-Persian troops fought nearer and nearer to his palace, Croesus decided his fate. Rather than suffer humiliation at the hands of Cyrus, he took his own life. Within hours the fabulous wealth of Lydia passed into the hands of the new emperor.

Before returning to Persia, Cyrus captured a number of Greek city-states that lay along the Aegean Sea. Then turning east again, he seized the parts of Syria he'd missed before and won the allegiance of many Arabian settlements along the border.

With all his victories, Cyrus still had control of his senses. He wanted to descend upon Babylon, but he didn't feel that his men had enough experience to face Nabonidus. So he returned to his homeland.

Back in Anshan, he took stock of the situation. He realized that many of the Iranian tribes of the eastern plateau remained free. What if they should attack Anshan while he campaigned elsewhere? He wanted to assure the safety of his own people. So he led his army across the high plains, subduing every clan as he went.

Within months, he had conquered Bactria and all the other truly Iranian outposts as far as the Cophen River. Standing on that river's shores, he even considered crossing into Indian territory. Then he remembered that Babylon was his main objective and decided to leave the Indians for a later time—if at all.

Wherever he went, after conquering a nation or tribe, he sought to win their loyal support by making them a part of his empire. He also gathered volunteers for his army, which, by now, had developed into an enormous fighting force.

The Persian king spent more than a year subduing the Iranian plateau, but now his thoughts returned to Babylonia. "Akkad is the breadbasket of the world," he told his war council one day. "That land has everything it needs to support itself—and many other nations too."

"Their farms grow huge amounts of dates and barley," added the chamberlain, "while their unending pastures feed enormous flocks and herds."

The Persian king glanced out the opening in his royal tent. "We need all those things to cement our empire together." He paused, deep in thought. "I have in mind," he continued, "something vastly superior to any empire of the past. I want to develop a super-international society. All nations will be free to live within their local customs, but they'll also trade with other nations. Everyone will have what he needs. When we reach that goal, all peoples will be satisfied, and we'll have peace throughout the empire."

"A worthy goal, my lord," applauded the general. In his mind he wondered what his army would do with no more wars to fight. "But my lord," he continued. "Babylon stands in your way. How . . ."

"*No one* stands in my way," interrupted Cyrus. The king's kindly eyes seemed to bore holes into the military man's face.

"Nabonidus has no one to help him now." He waved his hand in an arc to emphasize the size of his army. "He'll be helpless against so vast a force as this." He smiled as he turned to his officers. "So, gentlemen. Babylon will soon be mine."

"Catch those men!" bellowed Nabonidus. "We need them!" A lieutenant spurred his horse after the fleeing soldiers while the king turned to another officer nearby. "Organize those stragglers!" he barked. "Get them back into line. We've got to prevent a full-scale rout!"

Nabonidus cursed his gods. He'd returned from Tema only a few months ago because of Cyrus's encroachment upon his empire. The Persian king had conquered most of Arabia before advancing toward Babylonia. The territory over which Nabonidus had fought for years had fallen to his enemy in a matter of weeks.

Now, he and his generals worked feverishly to collect the fleeing remnants of their once-proud army. If only I knew more about warfare, he agonized. Nebuchadnezzar trained me as a diplomat, not as a soldier.

His work of regrouping became all the more difficult because of the waves of Media-Persian commandos lapping close at his heels. Cyrus had the advantage in both numbers and military genius. Another king might have saved the day; but Nabonidus was no Nebuchadnezzar. Even his most able generals faltered for lack of strong leadership.

When Nabonidus returned from Tema, he found his once-prosperous kingdom falling apart. The administration of Belshazzar reeked with misrule and graft. The son of Nabonidus, instead of protecting and encouraging the peasants, oppressed them with heavy taxes and his own personal plots to take away their lands. In their discouragement, these poor farmers had given up cultivating their fields, and now the once-fertile Babylonia faced the threat of starvation.

Though furious, Nabonidus had no time to repair the

damage, for Cyrus had entered his territory and now marched toward Babylon. So in the midst of his country's deterioration, the king had to muster his forces and prepare them to fight against overwhelming odds.

He soon discovered that Belshazzar's crimes had not been the only source of Babylonian unrest. The common people had come to dislike Nabonidus too. They hated him because of his decree canceling the religious festivals, his lengthy absence, and because he required everyone to worship the god, Sin.

In addition, Belshazzar's selfish policies had created a financial recession, and many people had lost their fortunes. Nabonidus had been out of reach, and the king's son didn't care about the needs of the people. These conditions had fueled the flame of hatred until the citizens had drawn near to open revolt.

Nabonidus himself lighted the final fuse of unrest by his treatment of the city's nobles. These men belonged to the privileged class—wealthy, famous, their lives filled with ease and pleasure. When Nabonidus began his desperate preparation of city defenses for invasion, he pressed everyone into forced-labor gangs—even the nobles. Some people smiled and considered it fair "justice." But many felt different. Forcing nobles to work struck at the heart of their culture and threatened to unravel the essential web of Babylonian society.

Nabonidus came to realize how the people felt and tried to rebuild his tattered image by proclaiming a New Year's festival. The troops rejoiced, and wine flowed like water for everyone. The priests removed Bel and Nebo from their temples, tied them to the backs of animals, and rode them through the streets. The entire city cheered that once again they could enjoy the most important ceremony of their religion.

But the king and the priests of Marduk found no joy in the event. They spent the entire festival arguing theology—which god was greater, Marduk or Sin. The prelates of Marduk hated Nabonidus because he didn't support their deity as previous kings had done. Instead, he had elevated Sin to the position of chief god in the national pantheon.

Everywhere the cauldron of revolt seethed, and Nabonidus worked frantically to win back popular support. He knew that Babylon had no chance in a war against Cyrus unless he could bring them all into unity.

All his efforts proved too little, too late, and when he marched north to meet Cyrus, few Babylonians wished him well. "Nabonidus delivered us into the hands of his perverted son for more than ten years," they reasoned. "Wouldn't Cyrus make a better ruler than he?"

Advancing to meet his enemy, Nabonidus reached the city of Opis before Cyrus's army arrived. He hoped to organize the city's defenses, but the citizens resisted. The people despised Nabonidus for the same reasons those in Babylon hated him, but they had further grievances.

Just before he came to Opis, the old king had ordered his men to rob their temples. He had stolen their gods and transported them to Babylon so that the Opis deities could defend the capital city. Now, as the greatest threat in their history bore down upon them, the inhabitants of Opis felt defenseless.

A large crowd gathered in the square opposite the main gate. They fumed as Nabonidus and his soldiers entered the city in the gathering twilight. Tension mounted. Dialogue became heated. Anger toward Nabonidus escalated into a seething fury. The crowd grew, and thousands began to vent their hostile emotions, at last evolving into an uncontrollable mob.

"Go home, Nabonidus!" shouted an angry voice. "We don't want you here."

"Give us back our gods," cried another.

"We want Cyrus," taunted a third.

Enraged voices swelled to an uproar, chanting: "Go home, Nabonidus! We want Cyrus! Go home, Nabonidus! We want Cyrus!"

The king scowled. Hungry and tired from the long forced march, Nabonidus felt fear begin to squeeze his heart. Cyrus offered him the most terrifying threat of his life, and now his own people mutinied against him. Panic pressed at his temples, paralyzing his reasoning. He struggled with nightmarish scenes of personal torture at the whim of a menacing mob.

"Hear me! Hear me, my people!" he cried, trying to reason with them. His voice vanished among the cascades of angry shouts.

Repeatedly he sought to gain their attention, but in vain. Each time he spoke, the mob's fury escalated, until they began to push in his direction. Sticks and stones flew at him, and his bodyguard moved into defensive position. Tension in the royal brain increased to the snapping point, and the king lost his nerve.

"Stop them!" he cried to his general. "Cut them down."

The hardened military man stood in his stirrups for a moment, petrified. "Kill our own people?" he gasped. "We need them to fight Cyrus."

But Nabonidus, like the mob, could no longer reason. "I'll have your head if you don't," he screamed as he dodged a stone that narrowly missed his face. "*Do it now!*"

Orders passed quickly along the lines, and troopers moved into action. Babylonian steel flashed like hundreds of sickles. Men, women, and children perished in agony from the deadly thrusts of Nabonidus's killing machine. The square filled quickly with lifeless bodies awash in blood as the merciless massacre took its course.

Shouts of anger turned to screams of fear and pain. Hundreds, thousands fell to the mowing machine of the mad monarch. The wounded cried for help, but no one answered, and most died before morning.

Remnants of the mob fled in all directions, and Nabonidus called off his men. His anger cooled, and reason returned. As he perceived the carnage his command had caused, he recoiled at his own lethal insanity. What have I done? he cringed. I've nearly wiped out the whole city!

By dawn, the metropolis lay ghostly quiet. Here and there the silence gave way to the moans of the wounded and the distant wailing of a handful of survivors.

The drumming of horse's hooves riddled the gloom, pounding to a halt just outside the main gate.

"One of our scouts!" shouted a watchman.

"Let him in," replied a nearby officer.

"Cyrus's army is but a few miles away, my lord." The scout bowed to the king from his saddle. His face grew pale as he looked around at the squareful of corpses, and his voice quavered. "They should reach Opis by midday."

As though in a trance, Nabonidus heard the message but couldn't tear his gaze from the gory scene around him. Blackening bodies lay everywhere. Men and older boys who might have added strength to his army now lay lifeless on the pavement. Their twisted bodies already swelled from the heat of the morning sun.

Nabonidus shut his eyes to the macabre sight. He felt faint, nauseated. Glancing back at the thousands who stood ready to defend his cause, he realized that they too felt demoralized by the meaningless slaughter of their own people. "There's no time now to clean up this mess and prepare the city for defense," he sighed, his voice whining like a naughty child caught in mischief. "Assemble the army on the plain north of the city. We'll have to fight Cyrus in the open."

The battle of Opis lasted several days, but resembled a massacre more than a battle. After years playing cat and mouse with desert chieftains, Nabonidus's soldiers had little experience fighting organized troopers. Cyrus's hordes pushed the Babylonians off balance from the beginning. They slaughtered Nabonidus's finest warriors within hours and soon had the rest fleeing for their lives, Persian commandos in hot pursuit.

"Let's regroup at Sippar," shouted Nabonidus. "Their strong walls should buy us a little time."

"Yes, my lord," agreed his chief of staff. "And their population should provide us with replacements as well."

Hours dragged by like days. Frantic officers on horseback attempted to organize their fleeing men into some semblance of order. Some stragglers needed the bite of the lash to remind them of their duties.

One unpopular general discovered that his troops refused to be begged or forced back into the war. As a last resort he and his lieutenants rode after them with swinging swords. They killed nearly half their company before the remnant cowered into submission.

Nabonidus and his staff reached Sippar first, followed at intervals by bits and pieces of their army. The soldiers drooped from the exhaustion of their ordeal. They needed food and water and rest among friends.

But the Sipparites didn't show themselves friendly. They'd heard of the massacre at Opis and had no desire to help a king who showed no justice toward his own people.

As Cyrus's advance battalions began to surround the walls of Sippar, Nabonidus realized he could never defend a hostile city. "We don't have a chance against Cyrus here." He sighed and wiped his eyes with the back of his hand as he counseled with his chief of staff. "Ready the men for travel," he ordered. "Maybe we'll find help in Borsippa."

Under the cover of darkness, Nabonidus led his loyal guards through the Persian lines and into the desert. "One last chance to save the throne," he mumbled as he spurred his horse into full gallop. "I must find another army. I must save Babylon."

1. Daniel 8:3-7.
2. Daniel 8:20, 21.
3. 1 Kings 8:46-50.

Chapter 5

Lower the River

"My lord." Gobryas bowed before his royal nephew.

"Uncle Gobryas." Cyrus extended his scepter, a royal gesture of goodwill. "I'm pleased to see you. Is your family well?"

"Yes, my lord. My family is in good health."

"What is your request, lord governor of Gutium?"

"Since my lord Cyrus graciously accepted Gutium [Elam] into your empire," he said, "have I served you faithfully?"

"Yes, Gobryas," returned Cyrus. "I count you as my most able governor and an outstanding general. Say on."

"It appears that we'll soon begin the siege of Babylon." The governor measured his words carefully, fearing that Cyrus might think his counsel arose from personal ambition.

"Your observations have been accurate." Cyrus smiled at the man who stood before him.

Gobryas had once been a general under Nebuchadnezzar. The great king had realized his potential and his fame as a brilliant leader of men. So Nebuchadnezzar promoted him to the position of governor of Gutium.

The Gutiumite had governed well, but Babylon's economic decay was sucking his nation into ruin. International intrigue and his own personal hatred for Belshazzar hadn't slowed the

63

oncoming disaster either. He had watched Cyrus rise to power. It seemed to him that an alliance with the Persian provided him the only safe way to withdraw from Babylonia without risking a major war with Belshazzar.

"What do you have to suggest, uncle?" asked the great king.

"Babylon is the largest city on earth." Gobryas drew from his intimate knowledge of its defensive structure. "I don't think we can conquer it with traditional methods like those developed by Sennacherib and others. We'll need to use a great deal of imagination."

"And a massive army, such as we have."

"Yes, my lord." Gobryas felt uneasy, even though the king was his nephew. He hoped that Cyrus would understand and accept his suggestions. "As you know, I spent many years in Babylon and led several army divisions in defense of the city's walls. I watched them build some of those walls and the canal system that surrounds the city."

Cyrus leaned forward, his interest growing rapidly.

"In recent years," continued Gobryas, "Nabonidus's wife, Nitocris, commissioned the royal contractors to dig a great water basin upstream from Babylon."

"Yes, uncle," replied Cyrus. "I believe she wanted to finish some of Nebuchadnezzar's projects."

"That's right," agreed the older man. "I think we can use that basin to help us gain access to the city. At any rate, I'd like to try."

"By all means." Cyrus smiled. "And if I remember right, you have a score to settle with Belshazzar, don't you?"

"Yes, my lord." Gobryas's face reddened at the mention of that royal rogue, but he suppressed his anger.

"I'll see that you have an opportunity for vengeance." Cyrus thought for a moment before speaking again. "Take a large force with you," he commanded. "Begin the siege and study the methods you think will help us gain entrance into the city." He looked away for a moment. "I'll round up Nabonidus and his army. Then I'll join you at Babylon for the final assault."

"Thank you, my lord." The uncle bowed. As he left the tent,

he stifled the urge to shout and clap his hands. Soon he'd have his revenge on Belshazzar. The son of Nabonidus would pay dearly for the crime he'd committed against Gobryas.

★   ★   ★   ★

Belshazzar couldn't believe his eyes. His personal enemy approached Babylon with an army large enough to capture the city. Retribution had come, and he shuddered with terror.

The middle-aged prince hurried back into the palace, still trembling from the awesome scene. All his boasting through the years, all his efforts to hide his crime and to quench his conscience—it all came tumbling down around his ears. His sin had found him out! His only hope for survival lay in the security of Babylon's walls and the efficiency of his army.

Slumping onto a bench within the security of his well-guarded throne room, Belshazzar lost himself in a bottle of wine. His world had begun to disintegrate around him, and his life appeared about to evaporate.

What will I do? he wondered, panic rising in his throat. Where can I go to escape the avenging angel of death? He could find no answers. But, oh, how he wanted to live! He'd callously taken the life of someone else, years before. But now, his own life seemed so very precious.

"My lord."

The king's son jolted with surprise and fear. He turned to see a royal messenger of his father's army, his uniform covered with dust from the perilous journey. Belshazzar didn't trust his own voice, so he motioned for the man to speak.

"Sippar has fallen, my lord." The page hung his head, his grief reacting upon Belshazzar, relieving his panic for a moment. "Two days ago," continued the messenger in a broken voice, "Nabonidus fled south with his army. He gave up the city without a fight. When I left him, he was moving toward Borsippa, with the Persians following close behind."

Belshazzar sat in stunned silence. He'd heard of the defeat at Opis. But it seemed absurd that the great Babylonian army would surrender a major city without a fight.

He waved the man away and began to pace about the

throne room. What should I do? he wondered. My father can't help me now. He felt abandoned. His father had shielded him from trouble all his life, but now the older man fled from Cyrus. Who knows? Belshazzar shrugged his shoulders. Father might even now have been captured and executed.

The defense of Babylonia now lay in Belshazzar's hands. Somehow, I must secure the wholehearted cooperation of the troops and the people, he reasoned. To do that, I'll have to obtain for myself a greater position of authority. But how? Almost everyone in the city hates me, and any sign of weakness on my part will provoke them to rebel. Belshazzar stewed about for an hour, mentally building one impossible solution after another.

"I'm lost," he mumbled as he sank down onto a bench again. Panic and anger again boiled up within his mind. "I can't see any way out of this mess."

"No, wait!" he shouted. At his sudden outburst, several servants dashed into the throne room, but he signaled for them to leave. He needed more solitude in order to formulate his plan.

His thoughts jelled within seconds. "I can save myself and the city too," he declared, smiling. "I'll take the crown and become the king of Babylon. In that way, I'll secure the complete cooperation of the people and the army."

"Page, come quickly," he called to the servant who stood just outside the door. "I have a message of great importance that will save our city."

The noisy nobles who had gathered in the throne room asked each other why they'd been summoned. No one knew, but all eyes darted toward the entryway when Belshazzar approached. Dressed in royal robes, he took his seat upon the sacred throne.

The whispering evaporated as the king's son began to speak. "King Nabonidus, my father, has suffered defeat in battle, and his armies now flee from Cyrus." His voice bore an authority the nobles hadn't expected from this spoiled playboy.

"It now falls upon me to govern and defend the empire," he continued. "In order to do this, I believe it imperative that I establish myself as king in place of my father. When I wield the royal scepter in my own hand, the people will rally to the defense of Babylon, and we will save the kingdom."

An audible groan rumbled through the crowd, but Belshazzar ignored it. He made it appear that he took this step in order to rescue the throne for his father. Secretly, though, he intended to assassinate the old man as soon as he could.

I will be *king* now, he boasted within his heart. No more of this co-regent stuff for me. I'll never again relinquish the throne to an absentee landlord!

Belshazzar pompously rose from the throne. "Tomorrow morning, I'll ascend the tower of Esagila to receive anointing from the high priest of Bel. Then I'll enter the holy of holies and grasp the hands of Marduk."

Two nobles near the back of the crowd held a whispered conference. "I don't like this," said one. "He has a lot of nerve to proclaim himself king while his father still lives." The noble adjusted his official robes as he talked. "And I've never seen anyone so poorly qualified to lead the empire. He never thinks of the people's welfare. He thinks only of himself."

"I know he's egotistical and inefficient," returned his friend. "But we don't have any other choice. The Persians are surrounding our city, and Nabonidus is in full flight." The nobleman pointed toward the Ishtar Gate. "We may have impregnable walls, but unless we have a wise king to rally the people and organize them, we haven't a chance. And don't forget," he continued, "Belshazzar is the grandson of Nebuchadnezzar—no less."

"You have a point," sighed his colleague. "But I still don't like it."

"Times can change a man," his friend replied. "The blood of Nebuchadnezzar runs through his veins. And Nitocris is the queen mother. She'll have a lot of influence upon all he does."

The two watched as Belshazzar descended from the throne and paraded toward the exit. "Perhaps he'll change when he becomes a god," remarked the first. "Perhaps one day he'll inspire an allegiance like the people gave his grandfather."

The royal coronation usually took place on New Year's Day—Nisan 1.[1] After a royal death—or when the need arose—the people enthroned a new king as soon as possible. Then they reinstated him again every New Year's Day.

The morning sunlight cast long shadows over the city. An elegant parade of nobles and officials led Belshazzar south on Procession Street toward Esagila—the sacred temple area. Years before, workers had paved the street with bitumen—a natural asphalt—while they added occasional glazed bricks for beauty. Yet potholes marred the once-elegant street, revealing that the son of the king had neglected his responsibility to maintain the city.

On either side of the street ran a 200-yard-long blue enameled mural. Each scene pictured a series of sixty multicolored lions. The effect still awed visitors, even though some of the tiles had fallen and others were marred.

The noble parade entered the courtyard of the most holy place in Babylon. The temple tower stood next to the sanctuary of Marduk, the Chaldean's dragon god. They often referred to the dinosaurlike creature as Bel—Lord of heaven and earth.

In spite of the early hour, hundreds of curious people crowded the courtyard. They craned their necks to get a glimpse of their new king.

Dozens of priests milled about, some fulfilling duties, while others merely stood around to see the curious sight. Most of the priests felt angry at the thought of installing this man as king. Like his father, Belshazzar had neglected to support their temple for the past ten years.

Throughout the crowd of onlookers, members of the king's royal guard stood at attention. They held their weapons drawn and ready for use in case priests or people attempted to stop the ceremony.

The spectators quieted when they saw a small group begin to ascend the stairs up the south slope of the 300-foot, seven-tiered tower. Black-robed priests led the way, flanked by two armed guards. Each holy man carried a pole topped with a gold symbol. The icon bore the shape of the letter T, with a circle superimposed over it—the logo of the sun god Tamus.

A nobleman followed the priests, carrying the crown of Babylon on a pillow. Behind him trailed Belshazzar with more priests, officials, and guards. The group had to step carefully, for some of the stairs had crumbled due to lack of repair.

Nabonidus had commissioned repair work on the tower during the early years of his reign. Yet the priests had done little to maintain the temple because the king hadn't assigned enough money to do the work.

The royal party ascended slowly. They stopped at intervals to test questionable footing or to allow the holy men to chant their incantations. At the summit, the nobles lined up on both sides of the stairs, facing the crowd below. Belshazzar knelt in the middle of the group, waiting for the high priest to anoint him and give him the crown.

The prelate scowled as he lifted the bejeweled diadem from its pillow and set it upon the head of the king's son. He bowed before him, and in a loud, hostile voice, charged Belshazzar to uphold the integrity of his office. Then he waved his hand over the new king, forming the shape of a cross and imposing the sanction of Tamus upon the coronation.

Belshazzar rose as the high priest approached again. The man chanted ritual phrases in an ancient tongue no longer understood by the common people. Gritting his teeth in anger, the priest swung his open hand in a wide arch to strike Belshazzar on the cheek—a coronation custom practiced for centuries. But the guard at Belshazzar's side intercepted the swinging arm. The sacred hand had doubled into a fist: he might have knocked the new king unconscious and sent him tumbling over the brink of the tower's sacred crest.

Belshazzar and the priest glared at each other, gritting their teeth like two dogs ready to fight. "I should take your head for that," the king hissed, but he quickly relaxed. "It's my coronation day," he growled, forcing a smile that twisted his face into an evil grimace. "I'll overlook it—today."

Belshazzar turned away, paused, and then glanced back at

the priest. "Perhaps tomorrow." Those nearest the king shivered at his guttural chuckle, for they realized that the holy man would soon meet an inglorious end.

The high priest demonstrated his personal hatred for Belshazzar one step farther. Stepping to the edge of the landing, he cupped his hands and shouted: "The king does not weep! Bel will not be gracious to us in the com . . ." He never finished the sentence. His face grimaced, his eyes became glassy, and he wilted onto the stone pavement amid a growing pool of blood.

Belshazzar's personal guard bent over the priest, using the prelate's immaculate robe as a rag with which to wipe the blood from his sword. Then he rose, returned the weapon to its sheath, and rejoined his master.

"Good work," mumbled Belshazzar, a smirk on his face. "Better have your men watch the others. They might try to retaliate."

With that, the new king carefully descended the stairs, strutted through the crowds, and crossed the giant courtyard to the temple of Marduk. He approached the dragonlike image of the great god and boldly grasped its outstretched claws. Now Belshazzar had not only become king, but had ascended into the domain of the gods!

Emerging from the house of Bel Marduk, he raised his hands above his head, expecting to receive a great ovation from his grateful subjects. Instead many people hissed at him, sticking out their lower lips in a gesture of disdain.

Belshazzar couldn't divorce himself from his past reputation. The crimes and excesses he had perpetrated upon Babylonian citizens while he managed the city for his father had won him no friends, and the people of Babylon did not want him as their king.

Back in the palace, secure from the anger of people and priests, Belshazzar began to feel his old self again. The bravado of former years returned as he laughed and joked with his officers and generals.

"Imagine the stupidity of those Persians," he scorned. "They come to the greatest city in the world thinking they can conquer it." He laughed loudly. "They can't muster enough men to even surround Babylon, let alone take it." (The city of Babylon had more than twelve miles of walls.)

"One of my scouts tells me that they've put some of their men digging ditches north of the city," put in a general. "They must have gone mad! Whoever heard of digging a canal when you're getting ready to besiege a city."

"Maybe they're making a swimming hole," suggested an officer. "Put in your time standing guard over the city, and then go for a dip in the pool."

The men laughed, masking their fear by heaping scorn upon the enemy. Inside, each had a knot in the pit of his stomach. Each had a fear that the Persians would break into Babylon—just as they'd conquered every other city.

"We need to celebrate my coronation," announced Belshazzar. "Every officer in the kingdom should have an opportunity to declare his loyalty to me as his new king."

"Hear! Hear!" cried the men in chorus.

"Chamberlain!" he called. The high official bowed before Belshazzar. "Prepare a coronation feast in the throne room tonight. Summon all the important officials: the lords and nobles and generals of the army." The king scratched his head as he planned the festival.

"Declare a holiday throughout the city. The populace should celebrate with us," he continued. "Supply wine in abundance for the army and those who guard the walls. Alert the musicians and the dancers to be ready for our amusement."

"What about Daniel, my lord?" asked the chamberlain as he mentally reviewed the guest list. "He no longer performs palace duties, but most everyone still considers him a noble."

"No!" shouted the king. "I don't want that Jew, or any other Jew, in the palace. Those swine should be eliminated from the kingdom, in my opinion, and I'll not have them or their God messing up my feast."

Belshazzar's face clouded over as he permitted his hatred for the captives from Judah to surface. He thought back to his childhood, when his mother had showed them kindness because of Daniel's close friendship with her father, Nebuchadnezzar. But Belshazzar had always resisted her.

The new king clenched his fist and continued. "Don't invite my mother either," he growled, as several nobles gasped. The queen mother had always been the honored guest at the coronation ball. "She's a Jew-lover," he accused, "and I want nothing of the sort at my feast!"

An evil smile played with the corner of his lips as he turned to one of the older counselors. "Didn't Nebuchadnezzar rescue some golden goblets from the temple in Jerusalem?" he asked.

"Why, yes, my lord," the surprised man returned. "They're on display in the palace museum."

Belshazzar spoke deliberately. "Place those goblets at my table tonight. I want to use them in making a toast to the gods of Babylon."

"But they're sacred," objected the old man. "It would be unwise to blaspheme any of the gods—even one so insignificant as the God of the Jews."

"I'm your divine king!" Belshazzar roared. "Are you accusing me of stupidity?!"

"N-n-no, my lord," wheezed the old man as he backed away. "I just th-thought . . ."

"Well, don't," the king barked. "I'm king, and I'll drink out of whatever goblet I please."

Gobryas surveyed Babylon as his troops surrounded it in preparation for the siege. What a city, he thought. None like it in the world. I wish I could reign there as king. The governor quickly jettisoned such thoughts. Fate hasn't given me the right to rule, he reminded himself. My work lies in serving another, and if in that service I avenge a crime—I'll be content.

Within hours, Gobryas realized how impossible it would be to surround the city's twelve-mile walls. He commanded one of the largest armies in history. Yet he couldn't put an adequate force around the city, let alone one with sufficient strength to storm the walls in a successful siege.

Gobryas called for one of his engineers. "I told you once that

Nitocris dug a large reservoir north of the city."

"Yes, my lord," replied the man. "She dug a man-made lake in which to store water to fill the canals during the dry season. I believe it was one of her father's unfinished projects."

"Yes," put in Gobryas, "and it's the dry season now."

"That's right, my lord. The river's at its lowest level during the yearly cycle."

Gobryas pointed toward the lake. "Nitocris designed the reservoir to empty into the canals gradually as the river fell. In that way, her engineers could control the irrigation of crops throughout the year."

"A terrific idea, my lord," replied the officer. "Nebuchadnezzar must have been a genius."

"The greatest of all time," murmured Gobryas. "And his daughter comes in a close second." Gobryas smiled. "If my calculations are correct, the lake should be about empty by now." He scanned a parchment scroll on which he'd written his figures. "The bottom of the lake appears a little lower than the bed of the river. We should be able to enlarge the spillway so we can all but drain the river into the reservoir."

"And lower it enough to march into the heart of the city." The engineer suddenly caught the spirit of the plan.

"Precisely," returned Gobryas. "We'll find it easier to capture the gates by the river, because they won't expect us to attack at that point."

He turned to his major general, who listened wide-eyed. "What do you think?"

"Sounds unbelievable," the man sputtered, still overcome with amazement. "But if the engineer can do what you're asking, we'll get into the city in a matter of hours."

"The river gates are strong," put in another officer, who had listened until now. "I lived in Babylon when Nitocris had them installed. They were part of her bridge project."

"Can we get in that way?" pressed Gobryas.

"We'd have a better chance at the river gates than anywhere else," the officer agreed. "They usually keep only a token guard there."

The intelligence officer entered the command tent and folded his arms. Gobryas motioned for him to speak. "One of my spies informed me that they crowned Belshazzar king this morning." He raised his nose as he spoke.

"King!" exploded Gobryas. "That rascal doesn't deserve to be an ash collector!"

The intelligence officer shrugged his shoulders. "He thinks it will strengthen his position and make it possible for him to resist us better."

Gobryas quieted, but his heart continued to seethe.

"You told us once," interjected one of his officers, "that Babylonian kings usually have a coronation feast on the night of their elevation to the throne."

"That's right!" cried Gobryas. "That may be just the opportunity we need."

"And didn't you tell us, my lord," put in his general, "that almost everyone in the city gets drunk during the coronation feasts—even the soldiers?"

Gobryas turned to his engineer, his voice vibrating with urgency. "Can you lower the river tonight?"

"If you'll give me enough men," returned the engineer.

The governor began spouting orders. He instructed his commanders to gather the most experienced fighting men to the place where the river flows into and out of the city and send the rest of the men north to dig the canal. Gobryas himself would lead the invasion, with the help of Gadatas—an old friend—as his leading general. All the diggers were instructed to rally to the fight as soon as they accomplished their task.

The air soon filled with shouted commands and the dust of thousands of marching feet. To mask their intentions, Gobryas had the men who waited near the river ports dig on the moat and erect observation platforms made of the trunks of palm trees. All the other men marched north, out of sight of the city, to divert the river into the lake.

---

1. April 22/23.

Chapter 6

Handwriting on the Wall

"If your men can't handle the job," Belshazzar fussed, "then get more men to help you. The feast begins at the ninth hour, and you'd better have everything ready."

The southern throne room buzzed with activity as the chamberlain supervised slaves and high officials alike. Servants hurried in all directions setting up tables, benches, and chairs for the royal banquet, while maidens hurried along behind them, decorating the positioned furniture. Tempers flared. Angry words and curses filled the air with tension.

The huge 174- by 56-foot hall was the holy of holies for the Babylonian government, but it also doubled as the center of royal festivities. The glazed brick façade had a black background decorated with garlands of yellow-and-white palmettos. Red-and-green columns topped by triple blue capitals added magnificence to the scene. A golden edge surrounded all the artwork, and a contrasting horizontal band of lions enhanced the effect.

One wall had a niche within which sat the throne. Beside this royal chair stood a pillar that reached three-fourths of the way to the ceiling. The pillar had a flat capital upon which servants had set several large oil lamps. These lamps gave light to all the room, casting a warm, rusty yellow glow over the entire enclosure.

Belshazzar watched several servants work with the palace engineer to prepare the lamps for the evening festivities. The engineer stood atop a ladder trimming the wicks, while a train of servants operated a bucket brigade to bring olive-oil fuel to fill an empty cauldron that supplied the lamps.

Belshazzar felt disgusted with the mayhem. "I wish we could find servants who would work efficiently," he whined to an aide. "Nebuchadnezzar's servants did ten times the work these are doing today." He turned to the beautiful woman who supervised the setting of tables. "Get a move on, you lazy, childless beggar!" he bellowed. "Your women should have completed that chore long ago. If you don't hurry, there won't be any food to put in your fancy pots."

The woman blushed and nearly burst into tears. Even though born of nobility, her life differed little from that of the palace slave girls. She remained childless because the king had forbidden her to marry. A lesser noble had repeatedly asked for her hand in marriage, but Belshazzar kept her in the harem as his own private plaything. Between orgies, he took advantage of her talents for organizing feasts.

The king saw a Jewish woman arranging wine jars in the corner of the hall. His sullen frown erupted into an angry glare. "Get her out of here," he shouted to the superintendent of female servants. "I don't want any of her kind getting in the way of my feast." He didn't stop to remember that the chief to whom he spoke—Meshach—was also a Jew.

Belshazzar became lost in thought as he reviewed in his mind the contact he'd had with the captives from Judah. During the time he'd been in authority, he had never openly persecuted the Jews, and yet he made them no concessions of any kind. They served a strange God, whom he refused to worship. In addition, his thorough knowledge of Nebuchadnezzar's occasional dealings with the Hebrew deity hardened him in his decision never to embrace their beliefs.

As his reign progressed, his hatred of the Jews had increased. Now that he sat uncontested on the throne, he felt a need to express open defiance toward Yahweh—in order to assert his own authority.

But his mother wanted to stop him. "You shouldn't forget what happened to your grandfather, Nebuchadnezzar," she often told him. "He resisted, and the Jewish God reduced him to a madman. If you respect Yahweh," she had taught him, "He'll strengthen you and give you long life and lasting happiness."

But Belshazzar refused to heed her warnings. He knew all about the illness that had overtaken Nebuchadnezzar in his final years. And his mother had often shown him a copy of the decree praising the Most High God as the One who "sets up kings and puts them down."

Nitocris's efforts only caused Belshazzar to steel his heart against the "God of creation," as she called Him. Instead, he convinced himself that Nebuchadnezzar had written the decree while he was still mad.

For all his outward hostility, Belshazzar had often felt a conviction that his own reasoning erred, but he loathed to admit it. He fought his conscience until now he no longer heard God's Spirit speaking to his soul.

Belshazzar's mind came back to the duties of preparing for the feast, and he complained again. "I need a sure way to win the loyalty of Babylon's great men." His voice whined while he talked over final plans with his chamberlain. "Some of them support me, but I don't trust the others." Belshazzar tramped around the room, biting his nails, scratching his head, and spitting on the floor.

I wish he'd stop that filthy spitting habit, thought the chamberlain as he grimaced. I don't dare tell him myself, but I wish somebody would. He's such an undisciplined imp! "I'm sure all your nobles will support you," insisted the chamberlain out loud. "They all know the Persians are preparing to attack our city. They know, too, that you're our only hope of rallying the army to fight them."

"Only hope, eh?" The phrase both pleased Belshazzar and rankled him. He liked the idea that he would become the city's savior, but he resented the thought that they supported him *only* because no one else could do the job. "Well," he bellowed, clenching his fist, "they'd *better* follow me. I'll take the head of every man who doesn't." No one who heard him doubted his sincerity.

★　　　★　　　★　　　★

The ninth hour approached. The lords and nobles of Babylon began to arrive at the banquet hall with their ladies, concubines, and personal servants. Palace butlers led each group to tables prepared especially for them.

"I don't like this place," shouted one of the nobles. "I belong at the king's table." The butler bowed but refused to move. "Take me to Belshazzar's table at once, you uncultured slave, or I'll leave!"

The chamberlain hurried to the scene with practiced grace. "You'll do nothing of the kind." He smiled, but squeezed the noble's arm until it hurt. "You'll sit where you're assigned, and be quiet about it."

The noble started to object, but he noticed the king's guards moving in his direction. He began to comprehend that pressing his importance further might incur the wrath of the king—something to be avoided at all costs.

Hot-tempered quarrels crackled throughout the banquet hall for nearly an hour before all of Babylon's important people found their seats. When at last the fussing flickered out, Belshazzar paraded into the hall. Behind him strutted his wife and concubines. The crowd rose as one man, bowed, and repeated—almost in unison— "May the king live forever."

Marching to the throne niched into the wall, Belshazzar ascended the steps to the royal chair and alighted with practiced pomp. The light from the great lamp stand at his side cast a warm glow over his features. Amid the gorgeous robes, the soft illumination, and the sparkle of precious stones in his crown, he almost appeared to have a handsome face. But the nobles all knew better.

A hush fell over the hall, not because the king appeared so magnificent, but because his mother hadn't entered at the head of the royal troop. Nitocris was the most illustrious woman in the kingdom. Everyone revered and trusted her.

She seemed to be the well of wisdom and power behind Belshazzar. She should have been the honored guest. But he hadn't invited her.

Belshazzar feared his mother's presence on this important night. She could draw the thoughts of lords and nobles back to Nabonidus, for the elder king still lived. At this moment he was hopelessly fleeing from overwhelming Persian hordes. But, by some miracle, he might yet save his throne. What then would happen to the boasting of his irreverent son and those who gave him their support?

The new king had another reason he didn't want his mother to come. He planned to magnify his own image by throwing public contempt upon the Hebrew God. Belshazzar had decided to use Yahweh's sacred temple cups from which to drink his wine. Nitocris would never stand for that.

He remembered how the great Nebuchadnezzar had buckled under pressure from Daniel and his God. But Belshazzar fancied himself made of sterner stuff. He wanted to assure his nobles that they could trust him to be strong and to serve the gods of Babylon.

Belshazzar advanced to his table—placed on a raised platform—and signaled for the feast to begin. Tambourines and pipes intermingled their audible vibrations with the haze from the olive-oil lamps and the aroma of cooking food. Scantily clad female dancers from the harem began to twirl around the tables, exercising their well-formed bodies for the amusement of the guests.

Nobles and ladies drank wine like water. Food floated to the tables upon large golden platters carried by costumed waiters. People's palates became awash with gourmet flavors, and their minds excited and dulled by the abundant wine. The eyes and ears and hearts of men began to covet for themselves the dancing girls who swayed to the hypnotic rhythms of Eastern music.

"Now's the time," said Belshazzar. "Bring out the Jewish sacred vessels."

"Are you sure, my lord?" asked the chamberlain.

"Of course, I'm sure," snapped the king. "I'm the god-king of

Babylon. I'm more powerful than all the gods in the world."
He cackled at his own joke while the drunken eyes of several
nobles drifted his way and wondered what he found so amusing.

"May I have your attention, please." Belshazzar became his
own herald, for he thought the announcement too important to
entrust to lesser persons. "My servants are passing to you
some of the most beautiful vessels in the empire."

The music stopped, and the dancing girls breathed a sigh,
happy for a moment of rest. "Ooos" and "Ahhs" arose from the
guests as they examined the golden vessels placed on their
tables.

"Where did these come from?" cried a noble's wife.

"They're lovely," squealed another, holding it up to the
light.

Belshazzar was irritated by the interruptions, but he
waited for the excitement to subside. "Nebuchadnezzar
brought these goblets from the temple of Yahweh in Jerusalem. They once belonged to the great God who—ha ha—we
are told, and this sounds so incredible, ha ha ha—was supposed to have made heaven and earth." His voice pulsated
with scoffing disbelief.

"We know our gods are greater than Yahweh!" he thundered. "We conquered Yahweh's people. We plundered His
holy temple." He expanded his chest and lifted his nose in
disdain. "Some God He turned out to be. He couldn't even
protect His own people—or His own temple."

The king's irreverent remarks brought forth an uproar of
laughter from his inebriated guests.

Belshazzar waited for the commotion to cease before he
spoke again. His eyes flashed with defiance: "Pour wine into
these 'sacred' vessels, my lords and nobles," he commanded,
finding it difficult to control his chuckling. "Drink from the
goblets of God." He lifted his cup high and shouted over the
rising din: "Praise to Bel Marduk, god of gods and lord of
lords. Praise to Sin, god of the moon. Praise to . . ."

An audible gasp ricocheted through the hall, drowning
Belshazzar's toast in midsentence. Hundred of trembling

hands replaced the sacred vessels onto their tables, pushing them as far away as they could reach. Some servants carrying wine pitchers lost their grip, dropping their containers. The vessels shattered, splattering Babylon's vintage all over the polished tile floor.

Belshazzar turned to see what caused the commotion. Some of his nobles pointed upward, their countenances appearing as though they'd seen a ghost.

The king's eyes followed their wild stares. What he saw might as well have been a ghost. Suspended in the air opposite the giant lamp stand appeared a pale, luminous hand, utterly detached from a body. It seemed to be twice the size of any man's hand. Fully formed, the hand had fingernails, and its knuckles were sharply defined. White hair curled outwardly from the surface of its gray-white skin.

Belshazzar's face drained of color, his knees lost their strength, and the sacred goblet dropped into his lap, spilling its contents onto his robes. He neither noticed the cup nor attempted to retrieve it. His eyes seemed riveted to the terrifying hand.

The spooky fingers went into action with a slow but resolute grace. Its movements gave it the appearance of being attached to an arm—and a body! Everyone in the room held his or her breath, praying to their gods that the hand wouldn't descend upon them. It seemed that judgment day had come, and the hand would sweep them all into eternity.

Instead of attacking the people, however, the extremity formed into a fist with its index finger extended. It moved toward the plaster wall above the glazed tile and began to write letters against the white background. The letters burned into the plaster, blazing as though fire emanated from the wall. Slowly, deliberately, the finger continued its work. The letters became words, but they belonged to a foreign tongue, and no one in the hall could read them.

Belshazzar sat at his honored table, but all thought of the festive occasion had disappeared. He couldn't take his eyes off the hand and the neon letters it traced on the throne-room wall.

When the hand finished its work, it slowly faded from view, but everyone felt a divine presence lingering in the hall.

Belshazzar especially felt overwhelmed as his conscience flooded his soul with memories of his evil past. It seemed that every wicked deed of his life crowded on center stage in his mind. He vividly remembered his dishonesty, his crimes—adultery, theft, murder. All his sins seemed to revolve around one monstrous outrage: his desire to persecute the Jews and blaspheme their God. The weight of his sins seemed heavier than he could bear, and his heart filled with abject terror.

The revelry ceased. Everyone sat in his place, suffering from shock, calling upon his own gods to save him.

Guests and servants and harem girls became seized with a horrifying dread. No one had the strength to flee. Each observer saw a panoramic view of the evil deeds in his/her life. Each individual stood alone before the judgment bar of the eternal God—whose power they had so recently defied.

A few moments before, the crowd had been laughing and telling irreverent jokes. Now many sat or stood in silence, faces pale, some gasping out choked cries of alarm.

Belshazzar regained some control and attempted to read the writing, but he couldn't. A wave of terror swept over his soul again, and he cried out, "Can't someone help me! Where are my counselors?"

Most of his counselors—the Chaldeans, soothsayers, and astrologers—sat as though glued to their seats, overcome by fears of their own. The king's command, however, shattered their inertia, and they stumbled toward the royal table.

Because of their own fears and drunkenness, these men displayed none of their usual dignity. Teetering on the brink of personal disaster, they held on to the table to keep from falling as they tried in vain to concentrate.

The king's counselors should have been able to read the letters without difficulty. They knew many languages and had often shown their skill in deciphering messages of this kind. But the eye of guilty conscience stared them in the face, and the effects of drinking all that wine added to their confusion as well. None of them could make any sense of the mysterious letters. The fist of fear tightened its grip on Belshazzar's abdominal organs.

Nitocris had mixed emotions about remaining in her private chambers. She felt humiliated that her son had refused to invite her to the coronation feast, yet she didn't like these affairs either. The drunkenness, the obscene language, and the dancing arrays of so many near-naked female bodies always sickened her.

This feast is important, she thought. This marks the ascension of *my* son to the throne of his father. He may be premature in his grasp for power. (She desperately hoped her husband would escape the Persians and come home—she loved him!) And yet, she thought, as queen mother I'll receive more public notice than when I was merely the wife of the king.

She'd always coveted power in Babylonian affairs. I *need* authority, she dreamed, so I can do the work I want to do. She'd already done more than any Chaldean queen in history, and she'd completed most of Nebuchadnezzar's unfinished ventures.

But as queen mother, she thought, I'll be able to do even more. I have several projects my father never thought of. With my new position, I'll . . .

Shouts and cries coming from the throne room disrupted her reverie. She felt the terror in their voices. At first she thought Persians had broken into the city and even now had begun slaughtering the guests at the ball.

She ran to the window overlooking the courtyard and peered toward the throne-room entrance that lay diagonally across from her quarters. Not a Persian in sight. She listened to the bedlam and watched the doorway for more than a minute. She heard no clash or arms, saw no guests fleeing from the exits. What could be the trouble?

Dashing down the broad stairway, Nitocris turned right and jogged through the now-unguarded throne-room entrance. She halted abruptly, taking in the scene. The room crawled with hysterical people totally overcome by the horror of the glowing letters on the far wall.

"It's judgment day," screamed a woman not far away. "The gods have come to judge us, and we're all lost!" She grasped her husband so tightly that the poor man couldn't have moved if he'd wanted to. As it was, his head lay on the table in a drunken stupor, vomit trickling off the eating surface into his lap.

Others cursed the king and his nobles. "We'd have lived better lives," yelled one lord, "if you'd given us a better example. Now we're all lost."

Nitocris glanced toward her son. He seems the most terrified of all, she thought. And no wonder. If this is judgment day, he has more to pay than anyone else. He knew better.

The queen mother picked her way through the writhing bodies of panic-stricken guests, carefully stepping over the remnants of broken dishes, spilt wine, and vomit. The din of excited voices gave way to an uneasy calm as she approached the royal table, but Belshazzar took no notice. The king and his wise men still gawked at the writing. Their minds hung heavy with the guilt of myriad crimes, and all their educated reasoning became tangled into knots of confusion.

As Nitocris looked around the room, her eyes lighted on many golden cups that lay on the tables. Memory stirred deep within her brain, while eddies of mental imagery lapped at the shores of her consciousness. She'd seen those lovely goblets somewhere before—yes! She'd seen them in her father's museum!

The sudden recollection jarred her as though an arrow had pierced her heart: "Those are Yahweh's sacred vessels," she said out loud. "Oh, no!" she cried, for in that instant she realized that her son had blasphemed the great God of heaven, the Creator of all things.

"He's gone too far," she moaned. And from what she saw, retribution already stalked him—and the nation as well.

Through tear-dimmed eyes Nitocris examined the letters still glowing on the plaster wall. God must have written them with His own finger, she thought. All is lost. My self-willed son is taking the whole empire down with him.

Suddenly her mind recalled the face of a man she'd first met more than half a century ago. "Daniel," she whispered. "If Daniel were here, he could read the writing. Perhaps, he could even save my son—and the kingdom."

"O king, live forever!" she exclaimed. Belshazzar's hopeless, wine-dulled eyes swung slowly in her direction. For a moment he gazed at the woman who stood before him, trying to connect her with the nightmare that surrounded him. Her simple beauty and high moral standards seemed vastly out of place amidst the debauchery of the past few hours. He required several minutes to recognize his own mother.

"Don't be alarmed," she said calmly. "Don't look so pale."[1]

She slipped to his side and wiped his forehead with the fold of her robes. "There is a man in your kingdom who has the spirit of the holy gods in him." She spoke quickly and softly, but with enough force that guests sitting at nearby tables heard.

"King Nebuchadnezzar, your [grand] father—your [grand] father the king, I say—appointed him chief of his court advisors. This man Daniel, whom the king called Belteshazzar, has a keen mind, knowledge, and understanding. He also has the ability to interpret dreams, explain riddles, and solve difficult problems. Call for Daniel, my son," she insisted, "and he'll tell you what the writing means."

"Daniel?" groaned Belshazzar. "I hate Daniel! I sent him away—he's not here—not in Babylon, anyway."

"Yes, he is," persisted Nitocris. "He lives near the palace. I saw him only yesterday."

A frown crept over Belshazzar's face, but it soon melted into an expression of hope—mixed with embarrassment and chagrin. How could he call on a man whom he'd dismissed in dishonor? And yet Daniel seemed his only chance. He shrugged his shoulders, turned his palms up, and spoke to the page at his side. "Send for Daniel," he sighed. "Bring him here at once."

Belshazzar, weak and frustrated, buried his face in his hands for many minutes. "This isn't how it's supposed to go at all," he groaned. All the expectations of pomp and glory he'd wanted to feel on this, the most important night of his life, had evaporated into a horror show. Now he had to kowtow to a man he'd hated all his life. Oh, the shame, he thought. If I survive the night, I'll never live it down!

The rising prattle of thousands of excited voices caused the king to glance up from his gloom. Daniel had arrived. Though in his eighties, the man of God exuded a radiant appearance as he made his way toward the royal table. The softness of his skin, the spring in his step, the ring in his voice, contrasted sharply with the drunken manners of those already in the room.

"Are you Daniel?" he heard himself ask. "Are you one of the exiles my [grand] father the king brought from Judah?"

Daniel nodded.

"I have heard that the spirit of the gods is in you and that you have insight, intelligence and outstanding wisdom." Am I really saying this? Belshazzar wondered in disgust. He seemed to have lost control of himself.

"The wise men and enchanters came before me to read this writing and tell me what it means." He spoke with a loud, trembling voice. "They couldn't explain it. Now I've heard that you're able to give interpretations and to solve difficult problems. If you can read this writing and tell me what it means, I'll clothe you in purple and have a gold chain placed around your neck and make you the third highest ruler in the kingdom."

Belshazzar felt mortified. Without so much as asking Daniel's price, he'd all but given the kingdom into Jewish hands. And he'd done it before thousands of witnesses as well. He couldn't understand why his mind caused him to act in this way.

Daniel smiled at the king—not from humor or conquest, but from pity for a man who'd sold his soul for fleshly lusts and the greed for power. "Keep your gifts for yourself," he chided, with a wave of his hand. "Give your rewards to someone else."

He turned to look at the still-glowing letters on the opposite wall. "Nevertheless," he sighed, "I'll read the writing and tell you what it means."

The prophet studied the scene of chaos in the banquet hall. Where less than an hour ago all had been revelry and drunkenness, now he saw a sea of sober faces. Every eye in the crowd followed his smallest move. Every ear listened to hear the slightest change of his voice, for the people perceived that Daniel held the key to their survival.

He turned again to the throne and stared into the eyes of the villain. When he spoke, sadness seasoned his voice. Yet every word rang with determination, for he was the mouthpiece of the Almighty God of creation.

"O king," he proclaimed, "the Most High God gave your [grand] father Nebuchadnezzar sovereignty and greatness and glory and splendor. Because of the high position he gave him, all peoples and nations dreaded him. Those the king wanted to put to death, he put to death; those he wanted to spare, he spared; those he wanted to promote, he promoted; and those he wanted to humble, he humbled."

Daniel paused a moment but continued to gaze steadily into the eyes of the scoundrel who cowered before him. "But when his heart became arrogant and hardened with pride," he continued, measuring each word, "he was deposed from his royal throne and stripped of his glory. He was driven away from people and given the mind of an animal; he lived with the wild donkeys and ate grass like cattle; and his body was drenched with the dew of heaven," the words fell like hammer blows, "until he acknowledged that the Most High God is sovereign over the kingdoms of men and sets over them anyone he wishes."

Belshazzar scowled. He'd been fifteen years old when the great king had lost his mind. He'd often watched from a palace window, gazing in awe as his grandfather wallowed about in filth, eating grass and flowers from the garden.

His mother hadn't let him forget the lesson either. She'd retold the story many times, until one day he'd angrily warned her never to mention the subject again.

Daniel's voice broke the king's reverie. "But you his [grand] son, O Belshazzar—you haven't humbled yourself, though you knew all this." Daniel's eyes seemed to burn from an inner fire, and the king could no longer turn away. "Instead, you've set yourself up against the Lord of heaven. You had the goblets from His temple brought to you . . ."

How does he know that? wondered the king. He wasn't here.

". . . and you and your nobles, your wives and your concubines drank from those sacred vessels." Daniel's voice gained in amplitude until it thundered throughout the hall. "You praised the gods of silver and gold, of bronze, iron, wood and stone, which cannot see or hear or understand. But," he hammered his fist into his palm, "you did not honor the God who holds in His hand your life and all your ways."

Belshazzar felt the fingers of terror slipping around his throat as he realized the importance of what Daniel said. He expected at any moment that the earth beneath his feet would open and swallow him—or that lightning would streak from the sky and strike him dead. But nothing happened.

Daniel softened his voice and turned to the glowing letters on the wall behind him. "Therefore, God sent the hand that wrote the inscription. This is what it says:

'MENE, MENE, TEKEL, PARSIN—four simple Persian words.

'And this is what they mean:

'MENE: God has numbered the days of your reign and brought it to an end.

'TEKEL: You have been weighed on the scales and found wanting.

'PERES: Your kingdom is divided and given to the Medes and Persians.' "

Daniel turned to leave, but Belshazzar held up his hand. He felt humiliated before all his nobles. Both his mother and Daniel the Jew had rebuked him publicly for neglecting to consider the God of heaven in his plans. In his heart he hated both of them for it.

Acting more out of instinct than choice, the king sought to save his honor. He conferred the gifts he'd promised, placing the royal robe and the golden chain upon the one he'd always disdained.

Daniel didn't resist. He graciously accepted the robe and the chain and the title of "third ruler of the kingdom."

Third ruler? Nitocris, standing behind her son, rolled the phrase over in her mind. Today, Belshazzar made himself king, she thought. He shoved his father aside so that he could be first. Why doesn't he give Daniel the title "second ruler"?

She looked again at her son, and immediately she knew the answer. Belshazzar's spirit was broken. He'd chafed for years at having to play second fiddle to his father. He'd wanted to have all the power, make all the decisions, without having to defer to his father's authority.

Now when faced with a life-threatening event with which he could not cope, he no longer wanted to be first. He longed to pass the responsibility on to someone else. The ominous hand and the fiery letters had burned the rebel heart out of him. He wanted desperately to go back, to become a little boy once more, waiting for his daddy to save him from the awful scene.

But Daddy couldn't help him anymore. And at that very moment retribution scurried through the streets of Babylon, hastening toward the palace to fulfill its righteous task.

---

1. Much of the conversation in this scene came from Daniel 5.

Chapter 7

Uninvited Guests

All afternoon Gobryas had been a dynamo of activity. His headquarters crawled with messengers—coming, going, waiting, resting between assignments. Generals, lieutenants, guards, and servants all worked feverishly to finish every part of the preparation so the invasion could go forward on schedule.

"Any word from your spies in the city?" Gobryas shot back over his shoulder.

"Yes, my lord," replied his intelligence officer. "You were right, my lord.[1] Belshazzar has announced a coronation feast to take place this evening. He's declared this a national day of rejoicing that he has ascended to the throne."

"How could anyone rejoice over the coronation of a wild ass?" Gobryas shook his head. "When does the festival begin?"

"At sunset, my lord." The officer smiled. "The chief of supply is already sending large quantities of wine to the troops."

"How convenient." The governor grinned. "It's just a matter of time, then. Belshazzar's playing right into my hand."

Gobryas stared through the opening of his tent, admiring the Ishtar Gate, not a mile away. O Babylon, he thought. If only you knew the time of your visitation. You rest and rejoice while your captor is near. Tonight—you will be mine!

90

A messenger broke his reverie. "My lord, I have a message from the engineer in charge of the river-diversion project." His exact pronunciation and upright bearing marked him as a professional page.

Gobryas gestured for the man to continue.

"My lord, the engineer says: 'The army engineers have been working all afternoon. We do not have enough shovels or baskets to do the job properly, but many of our soldiers have shown great zeal. They are using their swords and spears for shovels and their shields for carrying dirt.'" He paused, according to policy, so the recipient would have time to think over what he'd said.

"Go on, man!" encouraged Gobryas. "What's the message?" The governor sometimes felt impatient with the traditional protocol of career heralds.

"Yes, my lord." The page seemed rattled by Gobryas's prodding. He raised his chin and continued, his demeanor as proper as before. "The engineer says: 'The men have been making good progress on the canal.'" His speed had not increased, nor did he show any interest in the message's contents or urgency. It seemed his only sense of responsibility lay in delivering the missive in the proper style.

"Well?" cried the governor, on the brink of anger. "Will they finish the diversion in time for the attack?"

The messenger paused and looked directly at Gobryas—contrary to communication protocol. He seemed visibly upset that the governor had interrupted him two times. "Yes, my lord, I was coming to that." His voice trembled with frustration, but otherwise he controlled himself like a professional—though his speed did appear to have increased. "The chief engineer says: 'We will divert the river about midnight. The water should drop to about midthigh in the deepest part of the channel.'"

"Good," barked Gobryas, waving his hand toward the door. "Now go give him a message from me: 'I'm pleased with your work, and I count on you to do as you promised.'"

"But, my lord," the messenger objected. "I'm not finished. The engineer gave me the measurements of the canal and the depth of the water in the lake and . . ."

"Thank you for your thoroughness." The coolness in Gobryas's voice could have frozen the entire reservoir. "I'll hear the rest another time. Guard!" The governor pointed toward the doorway. "See that this man has safe passage *out of camp*."

"Yes, my lord."

"Messengers like that get in the way of progress," groaned Gobryas before the man had even left the tent. "Why couldn't he have said: 'The river diversion will be completed on schedule. You can launch your attack at midnight,' or something like that. That would have been enough."

The governor turned to his chamberlain. "When he finishes delivering my message, assign him to the task of carrying letters from our common soldiers to their families back home. Those people will appreciate his exact communication."

The cupbearer/statesman smiled, but turned at the sound of footsteps approaching the doorway.

"Gadatas!" Gobryas seemed pleased to see an old companion in arms.

"My lord."

"It's so good to see you again, my friend, but we haven't time now for talk." The two stood silently for a moment, staring into each other's eyes. Though many years had passed since their last meeting, they seemed but a few moments. The two men felt the bonds of their friendship strengthen once more.

"My friend." Gobryas broke the silence. "We'll take Babylon tonight, and I want you to lead the southern force."

"Yes, my lord." Gadatas grinned at his good fortune.

"You'll need to leave now in order to reach the portal of the river south of the city in time for the attack." The governor traced the movement on a map. "Move upstream as soon as the river is low enough for your men to wade safely. I'll approach from the north and meet you at Nitocris's bridge. We'll enter the city by way of the gate on the bridge."

"Looks like a good plan," Gadatas returned.

"Be careful of bow-happy Babylonians," added Gobryas.

"You'll be within their range all the way up the river."

"We'll be careful, my lord."

"General." The governor spoke to one of his aides. "Introduce General Gadatas to the second division, and see them off."

As the two generals turned to leave, Gobryas took Gadatas by the arm. "We've had many good times together, my friend." He smiled. "Let's plan for many more. Agreed?"

Gadatas grinned. "You can count on me, my lord." He patted Gobryas's hand affectionately. "The city's as good as ours."

The sound of drunken singing wafted over the wall as Persian forces gathered by the river in the darkness. Stars, blinking their jeweled eyes, seemed to hang so close that any interested harvester could have climbed the tallest tree and plucked them out of the sky. The moon's slender crescent lay low over the western hills as crickets and frogs performed their nocturnal symphonies.

Gobryas moved silently from group to group, checking that each platoon understood its orders.

"My lord," whispered a platoon leader as Gobryas questioned his plans. "Your command requires us to enter by the bridge gate and move quickly to secure the third tower west of the Ishtar Gate." He recited his orders from memory. "On the way we'll subdue anyone we find outdoors. When we reach the tower, we'll destroy or capture the guards and take possession of the turret ourselves."

"Good," grunted Gobryas. He moved on from one platoon to another, listening to a recitation of each group's orders.

As the moon touched the horizon, Gobryas had returned to the river's edge. The level had fallen several feet since earlier in the evening, and the water line had shrunk far from the dry part of the bank. In the starlight he made visual calculations and estimated the depth.

"Stand by." His whispered order echoed back among the waiting troops.

Using the butt of his spear as a walking stick, Gobryas

moved out into the water. Slowly, feeling the river bottom under his foot each time before he put his weight on it, Gobryas reached midstream. The level of the water came only halfway up his thigh. Wonderful! he thought. Our time has come!

The sound of reveling and drunken singing grew louder, and Gobryas realized that the city had reached the point of most cordial "welcome" to his troops. "Let's go!" he signaled to his generals. "Move quietly—watch your step, there may be holes . . . and keep a sharp eye out for ambush."

With that, he set out, forging ahead of his troops, leading the way. He scanned the river surface for eddies that could betray sink holes and watched the wall for signs of defenders. He held his shield high in case some alert guard might shoot an arrow his way.

On they splashed in silence, hundreds of brave soldiers ready for battle but hoping to catch the enemy off guard. Step by cautious step Gobryas led the way. Nitocris's bridge loomed into view. There was no sign of defenders anywhere.

In spite of the infirmities of advancing age—he was sixty-two—the governor's ambition to conquer Babylon and bring Belshazzar to justice kept him moving. Years of soldiering in the field had sustained his strength, and now he put it to the test.

As he neared the bridge, Gobryas saw the southern division approaching from the other side. He examined the walls and piers for a convenient way to scale them. Near the place where the bridge joined the eastern wall, he found a narrow ladder extending to the road surface. Nitocris may have installed it for maintenance crews or for boatmen who needed access to the city—it didn't matter. It offered Gobryas his ticket into Babylon.

The Mede peered upward to assure himself that no guards awaited him and then began to climb. He had only cleared the water when a soft voice called him back.

"My lord," Gadatas spoke with great urgency. "It's not wise for the commander to lead. What if there's an ambush? How could we complete our mission without you?"

Gobryas felt his face flush with anger and embarrassment. He'd become so engrossed in reaching his goal that he'd forgotten his training and his common sense. He looked at his friend and the hundreds of veteran fighters who stood around him—all men he could trust. Nearest the ladder gathered the platoon he'd assigned to do this work.

Gobryas descended and stepped aside while the commandos scaled the ladder—knives between their teeth. They sprang onto the bridge ready to fight, but it was empty. No one guarded the overpass. The commando leader gave the all-clear signal, and the governor joined them, followed by a steady stream of soldiers.

The governor of Gutium peered through the darkness at the west end of the bridge, and his mouth dropped open in surprise. The giant cedar gates stood open. Not an enemy soldier was in sight!

By this time the bridge had become crowded with Persians, and more ascended the ladder every minute. Gobryas gave the order for the advance platoons to move into the city. Some would enter the old town while others stormed the new. Their mission: destroy any resistance, take possession of the walls and towers, open the main gates, and sweep out across the city to take control of every important area.

As the Persians moved into Babylon, they met occasional groups of drunken soldiers—singing and joking as they staggered through the streets. When the commandos approached, they mimicked the songs and jokes of their foes, catching them off guard. By the time the drunks realized that these were enemies, the Persians had either killed or captured them.

Within minutes, the forward platoons had cleared the way for Gobryas and Gadatas to enter safely. Surging through the gates with his handpicked men, the commander forged toward the palace while Gadatas and his troops advanced on the Esagila temple area.

Soon, Gobryas thought, I'll meet my enemy face to face. Then, at last, I'll have vengeance. Justice will have its day, and Belshazzar will be punished for his crime against my son.

The mammoth city of Babylon sprawled over several square

miles. Its immense size made communication between its far-flung neighborhoods time-consuming at best. Few Babylonian soldiers escaped the onslaught of the Persian commandos. Those who did found difficulty in getting any action from the drunken men they tried to warn in other parts of the city.

The entire eastern half of the old "inner" city already lay under Persian control before battalions on the west wall knew that anything unusual had happened. Babylon's fall resembled, as it were, a giant parachute as it flutters gracefully to the ground, touching first one edge, folding, flapping in the breeze, drifting—at last slumping to the earth—its purpose spent.

Though the Persians had secured most of the city, the palace still offered resistance. The guards at the royal gate were warming themselves by a fire. They too had drunk too much wine, but at least they had remembered to lock the palace gates.

When Persian soldiers appeared, the sentries rallied and attempted to fight. But the struggle ended almost as soon as it began—albeit with much shouting and screaming by the guards.

Belshazzar had just proclaimed Daniel the third ruler of the kingdom when he heard the shouts outside. He became irritated, thinking that the guards were abusing their festive privileges or that perhaps a dancing girl had slipped out to entertain them.

He sent one of his personal guards to quiet them down, and several servants followed out of curiosity. The king's guard surveyed the scene at a glance: most of the gatekeepers lay dead, and Persian soldiers sought ways to jimmy open the gate. No time to waste! he thought. I must warn the king! He turned about and dashed again into the banquet hall to spread the alarm.

The servants ran too, looking for some place to hide. One man, thinking only to save his own skin, opened a small gate and fled into the night—leaving the door open. Gobryas's men needed no invitation. They swarmed through the small opening and regrouped inside for the final attack.

The Persians charged into the festal hall, ready for any

resistance they might meet. Pandemonium broke loose. Tables toppled as guests clamored to escape death by Persian sword. Wine goblets jangled onto the pavement, their contents splattering on the glazed tile surface, causing it to become slippery.

Resistance in the banquet hall ended quickly as guard after guard threw down his weapons and surrendered. Few Babylonians felt inclined to sacrifice their lives for a scoundrel like Belshazzar. Some of the nobles and generals fought the intruders out of honor, but the odds were against them, and they soon tasted the sword.

Belshazzar, bewildered by the train of events, whipped out his dagger, preparing to fight his enemies. They ignored him and spent their time rounding up captives. They grouped soldiers into a huddle opposite the throne. They gathered the lords and ladies at the extreme end of the hall and assembled the concubines, dancers, musicians, and servants in still another area.

Into this scene of loss and horror strolled a tall, thin man, whose noble bearing marked him as royalty. He had changed from his soggy field clothes into judicial garb, carried into the city by his personal servant. The common riffraff among the Babylonians took him for Cyrus. Belshazzar, Daniel, and Nitocris knew better. Gobryas, governor of Gutium, had come to avenge himself for a crime inflicted upon his son years before by King Belshazzar.

Gobryas stood in the entryway for a moment, surveying the scene. He saw the captive people, the bodies of guards and nobles who'd resisted, and the tables and floor cluttered with the remains of what had once been a sumptuous feast.

He eyed the still-glowing letters on the far wall and easily read them—guessing correctly at their meaning. He recognized the old man who stood beside Belshazzar and suspected why the king had called him. He'd seen the wise man years before in Nebuchadnezzar's court.

Belshazzar's eyes met those of Gobryas but quickly glanced away. His world seemed at an end. Within hours of his self-proclaimed coronation as king of the world's greatest empire, he had suffered several serious reverses. The handwriting on the wall stunned him, his mother had scolded him, his highest counselor had berated him and judged him a total loss.

Now, after he'd given Daniel a position of highest honor, Cyrus's well-disciplined army—led by his own personal enemy—wrested his kingdom from him . . . and would probably take his life as well. Belshazzar's knees buckled, and he slumped to the floor, too weak to stand. He knew his end must be near.

Gobryas studied the three figures on the platform. Nitocris smiled at him, her eyes betraying a long-buried admiration for the hero from Gutium. Daniel revealed no outward expression but stood erect, confident that God would protect him or grant him grace for any trial.

Belshazzar groveled on the floor. "No!" he cried. "Not Gobryas! Go away! Go away! I don't want to see you!"

He covered his head—like the proverbial ostrich burying his head in the sand. Sobs racked his form as terror took possession of his soul. Saliva dribbled from the corners of his mouth into his beard. His pupils dilated, his nostrils flared, his mouth hung open, fists clinched and muscles taut.

Gobryas mounted the steps and upended the royal table, sending gold and silver utensils flying. He stood beside the king, sword drawn, his frame towering over the royal wretch. "So, Belshazzar," he sneered, "we meet again. Be sure your sins will find you out."

Turning to Daniel, the governor smiled. "You've served your masters well, Belteshazzar. I'll also have important work for you." He bowed to show his respect for the old man. "You may go, if you wish. You need not witness the justice I must bring upon this evil man." Turning to a Persian guard, he said, "Escort this man anywhere he wishes to go and stay with him to see that no harm comes to him."

★　　　　★　　　　★　　　　★

Belshazzar's mind race as he realized his peril. He remembered the first time he had seen Gobryas . . . a more happy time . . . about thirty years before.

Gobryas the Mede had been a famous general in the

Babylonian army when Nebuchadnezzar made him governor of Gutium. He had met with Nabonidus when the statesman had represented Babylon on a diplomatic mission to settle a war between Media and Lydia. During the proceedings, Nabonidus had become friendly with the Gutiumite and suggested that a marriage alliance would help to cement relations between their countries.

Nabonidus lusted for the beautiful daughter of Gobryas and wished he could have her for himself. But he knew that his father-in-law Nebuchadnezzar would be angered by such an arrangement. However, she would make a fine wife for Belshazzar. In return, he offered to give his daughter as a wife for Gobryas's oldest son.

The two high-ranking fathers settled the agreement between themselves, and Gobryas's son accompanied Nabonidus back to Babylon to make the wedding arrangements.

Gobryas had not considered the differences between Belshazzar and his father. While Nabonidus was a fine gentleman, his son had grown up a stubborn, self-centered snob who demanded his own way whatever the cost to others. Nabonidus realized the defects in his son's character. He hoped that marriage and other responsibilities would correct his spoiled personality.

The prince of Gutium soon recognized Belshazzar for the fool he was. He began to despise this two-faced schemer and decided to break up the marriage plans. He wanted to spare his sister a lifetime of misery with such scum.

The prince made a mistake, however, in telling Belshazzar how he felt and what he intended to do. The spoiled child of Nabonidus by now had become filled with lust for the beautiful girl who had so swayed his father's heart. He refused to allow anything or anyone to stand in his way of having her. When he realized that the prince would wreck the wedding, he made some murderous plans of his own.

One day Belshazzar made a proposal to the royal son of Gobryas. "I understand you like to hunt."

"Yes," replied the prince. "I'm one of the best hunters in Gutium."

"I'll bet you've never bagged a Mesopotamian lion."

"No." The young man seemed interested. "Do you know where we could find one?"

"One did you say?" Belshazzar laughed. "We have so many lions in Babylonia that one Assyrian king boasted he killed 970 of them in a single hunt."

"Really?"

"Yes. I know the whereabouts of a whole pride, and it's not far from the city." He put his arm around the prince's shoulders. "I'd be happy to help you get one for your collection."

The prince became excited and began laying plans for the hunt.

"We can't take anyone with us," advised Belshazzar. "The more people we have, the more likely the lions will run from us."

"But I'm used to having a hunting companion," complained the prince. "My guard has often gone with me. He's an excellent huntsman too. Can't I take him?"

"Oh, I suppose so." Belshazzar's tone of voice discouraged the idea. "But I'll be your companion. Two will be much more likely to find the lions than three."

The prince considered the idea. He felt a little uncomfortable with it but wanted the lion trophy so much that he ignored his intuition. "OK," he agreed. "You be my companion. We'll go alone."

Belshazzar smiled as the two rode through a southern gate, crossed the Euphrates on a ferry, and headed out onto the plain. His scheme was working better than he had imagined.

No one in Babylon ever found out the truth of what happened out there on the plain. When the hunting party returned, the prince of Gutium lay lifeless across his saddle, mauled by an angry lion. Belshazzar had torn his own clothes and put ashes upon his head to show his grief.

Belshazzar told the story many times: The prince had fallen off his horse when the animal balked at the charge of a male lion. The lion mauled him to death before Belshazzar could rescue him.

The prince's Gutiumite guard accused Belshazzar of murder, but no one listened. Nitocris felt uneasy about Belshazzar's story. It didn't make sense to her, but Nabonidus didn't ask any questions. Instead, he talked with the judge and bought a favorable decision. The local court declared the son of the Babylonian noble innocent and ruled the death an accident. Belshazzar got off without even a slap on the wrist.

Gobryas and his daughter were furious even while they grieved for their loss. They canceled the wedding plans, broke off the family alliance with Nabonidus, and swore vengeance upon the one responsible.

Now, thirty years later, Belshazzar had all but forgotten the incident. To him it had been only one of hundreds of crimes he'd committed through the years. But his memory brought it all back. Now the dead prince's father stood over him, breathing out the fires of revenge, and the finest troops of Persia stood ready to enforce his will. The person who'd devised one scam after another all his life now faced retribution from the governor of Gutium, and there was no escaping justice this time.

★   ★   ★   ★

Belshazzar stood before the throne clothed only in a loincloth. The Persians stripped away his kingly garments and bound his arms tightly together behind his back—the elbows touching—causing exquisite pain to flow throughout his body. His consciousness slid from side to side, making it difficult for him to concentrate. If the Persian guards hadn't held him fast, he would have been unable to stand.

One witness after another gave testimony regarding Belshazzar's heinous crimes. He repeatedly declared his innocence, but in his stony heart of hearts, he knew that each one spoke the truth.

As the crowning indictment, Gobryas introduced Belshazzar's murder of the prince of Gutium—the governor's own son.

"I call to the stand the captain of my bodyguard," declared Gobryas.

Belshazzar became agitated when he recognized the military man who came forward. He had been chief of the guards who had accompanied the prince to Babylon years ago. The governor spoke to the soldier before he began his testimony. "The official Babylonian record says that my son died 'by the claw of the lion'—an accident. Please tell the court what *you* saw."

"He couldn't have seen anything!" cried Belshazzar, numb with pain and exhaustion. "We were alone when I . . ." He stopped short, realizing that he'd already said too much.

"Belshazzar!" roared Gobryas. "You've incriminated yourself!" The governor's inner rage rose to the top and began to spill over. He grabbed for his sword as he bounded from the throne and had raised it above his head before reason managed to bring his emotions under control.

His nose came to within a hair of Belshazzar's, and the prisoner trembled at the blazing fire that burned within the governor's eyes. "But we don't use a man's own testimony as evidence against him!" He spat out the words as he slammed his sword into its sheath and returned to his seat. "Guard," he shouted. "Tell us what you *saw!*"

"My lord." The guard shifted his weight to his right foot and began to stroke his black beard. "When my lord, the prince, left the city with . . ." He paused and pointed at Belshazzar, anger twisting his face. ". . . with this man, my lord, I felt uneasy. I'd seen some of his dishonest dealings with his own countrymen, and I didn't trust him."

"Dishonest dealings?" asked Gobryas, regaining his composure.

"My lord, he lied continually to his personal servants and his own guards. I once saw him cheat one of his nobles out of the interest due him on a loan."

"Go on," prompted the judge.

"When they left the city," the guard continued, "I followed at a distance. They rode into the desert and eventually came to an outcropping of rocks that appeared to contain a cave. The two sat on horseback, side by side, whispering. Belshazzar pointed toward the rocks, and the prince seemed to gaze intently at them.

"Then I saw Belshazzar draw his knife and stab the prince—*in the back!*" He shouted, the fury painting his face a pastel pink.

He paused to regain his composure, but his anger and the bottled grief of thirty years overcame him in a rush. "The prince tried to draw his sword, but he lost his balance and fell off his horse. Belshazzar . . ." He pointed toward the defendant, barely able to talk, "that man deliberately trampled him to death with his horse!"

"Why didn't you try to save him?" Gobryas's heart ached as the father in him felt the old wound open all over again.

"I was too far away, my lord." The guard sounded as though he pleaded for his own life. "By the time I realized what was happening, the prince was already dead!" His voice rose almost to a scream. He clenched his fists to the sides of his head as though he felt it would explode. "I wanted to charge down there and kill him—wring his neck with my bare hands."

He sighed and looked up at the ceiling, licking his lips, trying to regain his composure. When he spoke again, his utterance rose only a little above a whisper. "But I thought you should know the truth, my lord. So I turned and fled."

"That will be all." Gobryas had managed to squeeze all emotion from his voice, and it flattened out into a monotone.

He turned to Nitocris, who'd been sitting in the seat of honor near the edge of the platform. Tears streaked her paper white face, and yet her bearing displayed nobility and grace. "My lady." The warmth had returned to Gobryas's voice. "You've heard the testimony against your son, the king of Babylon. Do you have anything to say?"

She slowly rose from her chair and stepped down from the platform, walking to Belshazzar's side. The moisture seeping from the corners of her eyes as she looked into his pain-racked face formed into great drops that meandered down her cheeks.

"O my son," she moaned, touching his cheek with her open hand. "You were such a disappointment to me—and so was your father."

She buried her face in her hands and sobbed, her body

shaking violently. Gobryas stepped to her side and supported her for several minutes. The banquet hall lay silent like a tomb. None of the thousand noble guests, the hundreds of servants, or the Persian soldiers who guarded them dared make a sound.

The queen mother quieted and looked again at her son. "I heard the loud arguments you had with the prince of Gutium." She spoke with an intensity that sent electric ripples up the spines of every spectator. "And when you returned with his body—I knew what had happened!"

Her voice choked as she continued. "But your father—he covered it up—he persuaded the judge to declare it an accident. They should have punished you then, my son—executed you for murder."

She wiped her eyes before she continued. "I didn't want you to die any more than Nabonidus did, but he never even scolded you. He was supposed to uphold justice, but when faced with the crime of his own son, he became corrupt."

She looked at her hands and touched her chest and neck—absentmindedly pinching her throat between her thumb and forefinger. "I loved both of you, of course—I still do. But your behavior in regard to the prince of Gutium made me lose my respect for you and your father as defenders of truth and impartiality."

Nitocris returned to the platform and slumped into her chair. She lowered her head and supported it with the palm of her left hand.

Gobryas stood before the throne. "You have heard the evidence against the defendant," he intoned, pointing his commander's staff toward the royal prisoner. "Belshazzar, I find you guilty of the murder of my son and of many other crimes against your own people."

He paused, looking around the large room at the mixed audience. "By the laws of the Medes and the Persians, I hereby sentence you to death for your crimes. Executioner!" He motioned to a soldier who carried a large double-edged sword. "Do your work."

A rising murmur of voices swept through the crowd as the

guards made Belshazzar kneel. He sat down on his heels, his head bent forward to expose the nape of the neck. The headsman raised his sword, grasping it with both hands, and held it—suspended for a moment—above the head of the former king.

Nitocris closed her eyes and covered her mouth with a handkerchief to stifle any scream that might try to escape. Her son—her guilty, foolish son—was about to die. She felt her heart would break. She wanted to cry out "Stop!"—to run to his side and take the blow herself, but she knew such efforts would be useless. Everything revealed about him during the trial had been the truth. He deserved to die.

The executioner's sword flashed downward, deadly accurate. It severed head from body with one swift stroke. The head tumbled onto the cluttered floor, eyes staring blankly into space. The body remained kneeling for several seconds before it rolled onto its side. Belshazzar was dead.

Gobryas spoke to the Babylonian nobles and ladies, the servants, musicians, and dancers. "I wanted you to witness this trial," he announced, "so that you might know that Cyrus and Gobryas believe in strict justice." He stroked his beard as he continued. "We've come to release you from the tyranny of your former masters, who held you captive to their command. You'll soon know what it means to be free."

The Median governor turned to speak to one of his aides and then continued. "It may take us a few days to bring order and safety to the city. I ask you to go to your homes and to stay there. My men will accompany you so you won't suffer danger from other soldiers you may meet in the streets."

While the executioner's men gathered Belshazzar's remains, and Persian soldiers began leading the people to their homes, Gobryas moved to the queen mother's side. "My lady." He knelt on one knee, took her hand in his, and kissed it. "We've both suffered the loss of our sons." He paused to allow his pounding heart to calm. "My heart aches for you just now, for I know the pain you feel."

Nitocris smiled through her tears. "When I was a young girl," she said, dabbing her handkerchief at moisture collecting in the corner of Gobryas's eye, "you were my favorite general in father's army. He used to tell me stories of your exploits, and I've always admired your bravery."

She looked away for a moment, swallowing the sob that forced its way into her throat. "And I've also admired your gentleness. I've known for many years about your oath of vengeance against my son. It was well-grounded, as everyone can see.

"But tonight you acted the gentleman in every way. You could have stormed in here and killed him with your own sword. You could have tortured him mercilessly like many conquerors do to their royal captives. No one could have stopped you.

"But you didn't do that. You held court so everyone could see that my son . . . ," her voice broke again, ". . . how guilty he was. Then you punished him according to the laws of justice."

Gobryas put his hand under her chin and lifted her head so he could gaze into her eyes. "You may remain in the palace if you like," he said. "You shall always have a place of honor—as long as you live." She smiled and nodded as he rose without further word, bowed to her, and left the banquet hall.

The once-flaming letters had faded from the wall, and the light from the lampstand flickered with the last drops of oil. Babylon, the joy of the Chaldee kingdom, the light of the world—Babylon had fallen, never to rise again.

★　　　★　　　★　　　★

Nitocris leaned heavily upon her maid as she left the disheveled ballroom. The shock and grief of the last hours left her aging body near collapse. At sixty-eight, she still wore a youthful figure, and the beauty of yesteryear lingered on her face. The worry of Belshazzar's delinquency, the separation from her now-fleeing husband—and the awareness that her father's beloved Babylon was falling into alien hands—had taken their toll.

In a small courtyard behind the banquet hall, she found Daniel. "May Yahweh bless you, honored lady," he said. "Your pain is too great for you to bear alone."

Nitocris stopped. She smiled weakly at her friend and motioned him to a bench near the wall. "What happened, Daniel? Why did my son turn out so badly?"

Daniel bowed before her and took her hand in his, seeking to comfort her grief. "Belshazzar was weak, my lady, and Yahweh knew his weakness." He wiped his own eyes as a teardrop began to form at the corner of his lashes. "Yahweh wanted to protect him, to help him make right choices, but he refused. He knew about God's power and greatness. He knew how God had humbled your father's heart. He was free to choose the right way—and Yahweh would have blessed him if he had."

The old prophet squeezed her hand. "When Belshazzar refused to serve Yahweh, he also rejected His protection. God gave him up to his bad habits, and these led him to become even worse."

Daniel looked away for a moment. "Tonight, when Belshazzar drank from the sacred vessels of God's temple, he not only desecrated those vessels, but he also profaned his own body temple with the wine he drank. He chose to ignore God as much as he could—to use the powers God gave him for feasting and drinking instead of for administering justice and mercy. God loved him more than you did, but He didn't have any choice. He finally had to let him go, to give him up to his own passions.

"So when the Medes and the Persians attacked the empire, God couldn't protect either your husband or Belshazzar. You saw the results of their decision tonight. I'm sorry you've been so terribly hurt by the wrongs of others."

"Thank you, Daniel," she said, squeezing his hand. "May the blessing of your God rest upon me."

---

1. The intelligence officer had originally presented the idea of the coronation feast, but proper court courtesy required that all correct decisions be applied to the ruler—in this case, Gobryas.

Chapter 8

The Liberator

"See that our men secure the city," ordered Gobryas, as he left the banquet hall.

"Yes, my lord," returned the general. "They've already occupied the towers on the northern wall and opened the Ishtar Gate. The diggers are beginning to enter the city now."

"Good." Gobryas thought for a moment. "We'll need martial law for a few days, until we disarm the enemy. Call a curfew every night at sundown. Kill anyone in the streets at night on sight." He scratched his chin through his beard. "The temple and the tower will be our biggest problem."

"How so?"

"They believe the god Marduk is the soul of Babylon. Zealous loyalists will naturally use his temple as a citadel from which to launch raids against us."

"I see what you mean," returned the general. "What do you suggest?"

"I think we should allow the people to worship as they choose," answered Gobryas. "Cyrus would want it that way. But . . ." he wiped his tired eyes, ". . . but have our guards collect their weapons before they enter." He raised his hands, palms up, in a gesture of futility. "No weapons? No war!"

★   ★   ★   ★

"He's a coward!" complained Cyrus. He didn't like that Nabonidus had given up Sippar without a fight.

"We gave him quite a pounding at Opis," reminded his personal servant. "He knows when he's beaten."

"Perhaps." Cyrus scowled as he searched the southern horizon for signs of the fleeing enemy. "But to surrender a major city without even trying to defend it? It doesn't seem true to character."

"If he hadn't massacred all those people at Opis," put in his general, "he might have made a better showing."

Cyrus felt a chill travel up his spine as he remembered all those bodies. Barbaric!

"Why didn't Nabonidus defend Sippar?" asked a lieutenant as he pulled his horse up beside Cyrus. "It has defendable walls and a sizable population—enough food and water for months of siege. I can't understand why he didn't stand and fight."

"Nor can I," replied Cyrus. "Unless . . ." He remembered how the people cheered him when he approached the open gate. They treated him like a—like a liberator! "Maybe they didn't like Nabonidus and simply refused to fight for him."

Cyrus moved south with his mammoth army, now including volunteers from Opis and Sippar. He had no difficulty tracing the fleeing Babylonians, for they had lightened their packs by throwing away everything they didn't need. Rubbish of all kinds littered the road that ran south and east toward Borsippa. The Persians could also see that most of the army had leaked away from the main division—deserting their king and looking for a safer haven.

"He's in there," remarked a Persian general, when they finally reached the walls of Borsippa. "My men have ridden around the city, and there's no evidence of Nabonidus's departure."

"Good," returned Cyrus. "Have your men set up camp."

"Yes, my lord," answered the general. "It doesn't look like Borsippa should be a hard nut to crack."

"How many men do you think Nabonidus has?" asked Cyrus.

"Couldn't be more than two or three hundred," returned the general. "A great many deserted him along the way." He gazed at the city wall for a moment. "A lot depends on how many Borsippians are willing to fight for him."

"Judging from the attitude we've seen toward him in other cities," commented Cyrus, "I doubt any of these people will join with him—voluntarily." He stroked his graying blond beard and put his hands on his hips. "If any of Nabonidus's men want to escape, let them go. Let's drain off as many as we can. In the meantime, prepare for a siege."

Babylonian soldiers escaped the city by the dozens during the first days of the siege. To make matters worse, Borsippians refused to join the king's fast-dwindling ranks.

"It's turning out just as I thought," laughed Cyrus. "Before long, he won't have enough men for watchmen on the walls."

A messenger from the north pounded to a stop not far from Cyrus's headquarters' tent. He dismounted and dashed to the spot where the great conqueror stood.

"My lord," he sputtered, bowing at Cyrus's feet. "General Gobryas has taken Babylon, slain the king's son, and secured the entire area." He stopped to catch his breath. "He awaits your arrival to occupy the city."

"Why, that wonderful uncle of mine!" exclaimed Cyrus, laughing. "It's just like him. I sent him off to begin the siege of Babylon so everything will be ready for me when I arrive. And what does he do?" He laughed again. "He conquers the city himself. What a man! Would that I had thousands more like him."

The word of Babylon's fall passed from one platoon to another until it had been carried around the city. A mighty cheer swelled through the rank and file. Babylonian soldiers peeped over Borsippa's bulwarks, wondering what their enemies found so pleasing. They didn't have long to guess.

"Babylon is fallen!" someone began to chant, and it soon echoed through all the Persian camps. "Babylon is fallen, is fallen, that great and might city! Hooray for Gobryas."

Cyrus listened to the chant for several minutes and then looked at his general. "We're wasting our time here," he observed. "Tomorrow morning, let's break camp and start for Babylon."

"But we haven't caught Nabonidus yet," the general objected. "What if he attacks us from the rear?"

"No fear of that," returned Cyrus. "His capital is gone, his friends are gone, most of his army is gone. No one wants Nabonidus anymore—let him go. He's of no more value to us."

The Persian army took its time marching from Borsippa to Babylon. The men rested often, renewing their strength in anticipation of any resistance they might meet along the way.

Rather than march directly to Babylon and enter its drab southern gate, Cyrus circled his army around to the east. He wanted to make a triumphal entry through the Ishtar Gate and parade down Procession Street.

"Army approaching from the north!" The watchman's cry came from atop the outer wall, a mile and a half north of the old inner city. His alarm was repeated by other sentinels until the news flashed all around the metropolis.

Within minutes a messenger entered a small chamber off the throne room of the southern palace, where Gobryas had set up his temporary headquarters. The governor spoke before the page could even open his mouth. "Does the watchman know yet if the army is friend or foe?" he asked.

"The watch captain thinks it's Cyrus," returned the messenger. "But I don't really know. Cyrus went to Borsippa, didn't he? That's south of Babylon, isn't it? Why would Cyrus come from the north?"

Gobryas smiled at the barrage of questions. "If you'd captured the world's greatest city," he asked in return, "and now you're coming to claim it, through which of Babylon's gates would you choose to enter?"

"The Ishtar Gate, my lord."

"Exactly." Gobryas rose from the couch on which he'd been resting. "Let's make ready for our master," he ordered. "Send heralds throughout the city, saying, "Cyrus the Great, king of lands, is entering Babylon. Come out and greet him. Rejoice, for your liberator is at hand!"

The young man disappeared. Within minutes dozens of royal messengers left the palace to announce the good news at every major intersection throughout the city. Everywhere they went, they spread the word that the world's greatest king approached Babylon in triumph.

By the time Cyrus entered Babylon, the city had been in Persian hands for two weeks. Gobryas and his men had destroyed every group that openly opposed Persian rule. A few zealots remained, but they found themselves isolated and without weapons or power.

Cyrus's horse pranced up to the Ishtar Gate, reflecting the excitement of his royal rider. Gobryas came forth out of the city, advancing to meet his master on foot. His personal servant followed close behind, leading the governor's horse. The Persian king reined in his steed, looked down at his uncle, and smiled.

"My lord," called Gobryas in a loud voice, as he bowed to his famous nephew. "I present to you Babylon the great, the pride of the Chaldees, the gate of the gods, the most glorious city to grace my lord's empire. May my lord, Cyrus the Great, king of lands, look graciously upon your humble servant and accept this gift from my hand." With that, Gobryas bowed, with his forehead touching the glazed tile surface of the entry road. He remained in that position, awaiting his master's permission to rise.

Cyrus felt a stab of jealousy. He'd wanted to take Babylon himself! But as he gazed at the bowing form of his uncle and at the loyal soldiers who had fought in the older man's army, all jealousy disappeared. After all, he reminded himself, Gobryas acted in my behalf.

The great conqueror smiled. "You may rise, Gobryas. You have served me well, and you shall be rewarded." He pointed through the gates. "Come now, my friend, show me the prize you've given me."

Gobryas mounted his horse and fell in beside—but slightly

behind—his master. The two leaders inched their way through the crowds of cheering people as they and their guards rode slowly down Procession Street. Many citizens cast green twigs into the street to serve as an improvised carpet over which the new king could ride.

As the party advanced through the city, the people's shouts began to blend, until as one voice they chanted: "Cyrus, liberator! Cyrus, liberator!" Some women became so overcome with the emotion of the moment that they ran alongside his prancing horse and kissed his dusty feet. Everywhere he looked, he saw beaming faces—jubilant people, happy that Cyrus had become their king.

"You've saved us," cried one man.

"You've taken us from death into life!" shouted another.

Cyrus had never before seen such enthusiasm, such welcome. Tears streamed down his face for the joy he felt inside. Here he saw living proof that he'd accomplished his purpose: he'd freed these people from slavery to their Chaldean masters.

After the royal band passed the temple tower with its sprawling campus, Gobryas led the group away from the crowded streets. They traveled along several back alleys and soon entered the southern palace.

As the Persian party dismounted, Cyrus sighed. His happiness seemed complete, but he felt exhausted from the buffeting of the crowds and the emotional high of the universal acceptance. "Never have I seen such joy," he remarked to Gobryas. "It was as though they accepted me as a god—as their savior from some terrible adversary."

"You *have* saved them," returned Gobryas. "Nabonidus didn't give them any real leadership. He issued his decrees from some distant city, knowing very little about the circumstances here in Babylon."

The governor paused and bit his lip in an attempt to prevent the churned-up emotion in his heart from overcoming him. "And Belshazzar." His pronunciation sounded like a growl. "He became one of the worst slave drivers I've ever known—oppressive to the core."

"That bad, eh," mused Cyrus. The two strolled across the large courtyard inside the main gate as the Persian king gazed around himself. He felt awed by the size and beauty of the place.

"Nabonidus wasn't always bad," continued Gobryas. "I remember him when we served together in Nebuchadnezzar's court. He was so warm and understanding—willing to go to any length to help people."

"I've heard you talk about him, uncle," put in Cyrus.

"Yes, my lord. But he didn't know anything about running a government," continued the older man. "He made a mess of things here in Babylon, and that put a great burden on the people." Gobryas shook his head as he went on. "He must have been out of his mind when he placed his hotshot son in charge of the city during his absence. That was a disaster!"

"It's no wonder the people rejoiced at my coming," sighed Cyrus. "They'd welcome anyone who promised them better leadership than Nabonidus and Belshazzar."

Gobryas changed the subject. "Come, let me show you around the palace."

Cyrus gasped repeatedly as he passed from one courtyard into another. Each of the five open areas seemed more spectacular than the last. When they entered the throne room, the Persian king stood silently, drinking in the beauty of the hall.

Cyrus, king of lands, slowly ascended the stairs of the grand niche in the throne-room wall. He deliberately took his place upon the royal seat of Babylon.

"It fits you well," cried Gobryas, clapping his hands. "Who would have thought that the governor of Gutium would have a nephew to sit upon the throne of Babylon." He laughed and danced about, while Cyrus and the guards grinned.

"Come, Uncle Gobryas," chided Cyrus. "We have work to do."

"Yes, my lord." Gobryas still felt giddy. "What does my lord nephew wish to do on this important occasion?"

Cyrus ignored the good-natured remark. "There's been too much war," he said. "Many homes have been broken by the deaths of brave soldiers. Hearts weep because of the loss of husbands and fathers and brothers . . ." He touched his lips with his forefinger and gazed at some imaginary object beyond the walls of the throne room. "I want to bring the suffering to an end. I want peace—a peace that will prevent war." He rose from the throne, descended the steps, and gestured for Gobryas and the court officials to come near.

"We must keep a strong army—ready to fight when it's needed," he continued. "But I want the soldiers to be out of sight as much as possible. I want the people to get used to the feeling of peace—to realize that prosperity has again come to their nation."

"That's a wonderful idea," put in Gobryas.

"Tell me, uncle," asked the king. "I understand that Nabonidus stole the gods from many cities and brought them here to Babylon."

"That's true, my lord." Gobryas's smile faded into a frown. "Just before marching to Opis, he brought all the gods here to protect his Babylon, so he said. He even stole the god from my temple in Susa! Right out from under my nose!"

"He did?"

"Yes. That was the last humiliating blow, as far as I was concerned. That's when I decided to withdraw from the Babylonian Empire and join with you. Many people hate Nabonidus for taking their gods like that."

"I would imagine so." Cyrus ran his hand through his wavy blond hair as he thought about what had happened.

People in Mesopotamia paid more attention to their religion than did almost any other civilization in the world. They spent huge amounts of time and money building temples and supporting the priests who served their favorite gods.

Each province had its own patron deity, and some cities supported several gods. When Nabonidus removed the idols, it had a disastrous impact upon the esteem of the people who worshiped them.

"I think we could gain favor with the people," continued Cyrus, "if we returned all those gods to their own temples."

"A good suggestion, my lord," returned Gobryas. "The Babylonians would never forget the kindness, even though it would seem a little thing to us."

"Then make it so," ordered Cyrus. "Take care, though," he warned. "Some religious groups may feel hostile toward us. Watch them closely so we can keep ahead of possible trouble."

The Persian stopped to think for a moment. "Place guards in or near all the temples—just for observation. Instruct them to be friendly and to leave their weapons at home, unless they have good reason to feel threatened. I want the people to know that we trust them. When they realize this, they'll trust us too."

The king strolled along the wall of the throne room, examining the intricate patterns of the mosaic pictures. "We know that Nabonidus has few friends in Babylon." He chose his words carefully. "But people may begin to sympathize with him."

"What do you mean?" asked his uncle.

"He's the underdog now." Cyrus turned to face the governor, gazing deeply into his eyes. "Some will forget his atrocities and seek to reinstate him, to put a Babylonian king back on the throne. After all," he added, "we're not Semites like them. We're Aryans—the first of our race to conquer Mesopotamia. They will surely think of us as foreigners."

"I see," sighed Gobryas. "What do you think we should do?"

"We need to discredit Nabonidus," suggested Cyrus. "If the people hear about his crimes often enough, they'll never forget his corruption."

"We won't have any trouble gathering fuel for that fire," laughed Gobryas. "He's left us dozens of horror stories we can use."

"Good," returned Cyrus. "Then we need only broadcast the truth. Soon anyone who supports Nabonidus will want to crawl into a viper hole and disappear."

"It shall be done." Gobryas smiled. "I'll see to it myself."

★   ★   ★   ★

A small, motley band of soldiers approached Babylon from the south. None of the observers atop the walls felt threatened by the group, but they wondered how these warriors had gotten so near without detection by peripheral scouts.

The riders appeared old and tired, and their clothes and horses were caked with dirt. Yet they sat in their saddles like kings going forth to war. They moved toward the open gate with measured pace in an effort to quiet the fears of the Persian defenders and prevent them from sounding a general alarm.

Nabonidus no longer felt like fighting or running or hiding. The day before, as he had paced about his headquarters in Borsippa, he had told his general, "It's not right for a Babylonian king to run and hide like a scared rabbit."

"I agree," returned the military man. "So why don't we go out and attack a band of Persians? Then we can all die bravely in battle."

"To what point?" asked the king. "Why should more people die, when we've already lost the throne?"

"Then what should we do?" asked his personal servant. "Should we just show ourselves and surrender?"

"Yes . . ." Nabonidus hesitated, unsure of himself but trying to hide his fears from those who had served him so faithfully. "Yes, we must surrender ourselves to the enemy."

"But they'll torture you and kill you," cried the servant.

"I'm sure they will," replied Nabonidus as he straightened to his full height. He had a faraway look in his eyes as he quietly considered what he planned to do. After several moments, he looked around at his loyal band. "I will die, of course," he said, "but you'll all live and return to your families."

"We'd rather die!" shouted the general.

The king put his finger on the soldier's lips. "Whether you live or die is a matter for your king to decide." His voice vibrated with a newfound strength and authority. "I want you to live, and that's the way you'll serve me best."

"Yes, my lord," they chorused. Their sense of honor was disappointed, and yet their hearts filled with gratitude.

Now, after many hours of exhausting travel, they rode up the last hill into Babylon. Their weapons remained sheathed, and Nabonidus's flag flitted atop the general's spear. They made it plain by their actions that they did not plan to fight. They had come to surrender.

Inside the gate, Nabonidus's dreary band continued along Procession Street. A mounted guard of Persian soldiers fell in behind, but no one stopped them or asked them, "Where are you going?"

The people who walked along the street stopped to look at the mounted group as they proceeded at a funeral pace. Some recognized their former king, and in spite of the inner hatred for his policies, they sympathized with his loss of the throne.

At the palace gates, Nabonidus and his men dismounted. They gave the reins of their horses to waiting stable boys and stood at attention facing the gate.

"We have come for an audience with his majesty, King Cyrus," announced Nabonidus's scribe.

Sensing the importance of the moment, the Persian guard bowed to the former Babylonian king. "Follow me," he requested, and turned to lead the group into the palace.

Nabonidus's heart felt heavy as he passed through one courtyard after another. Once in the throne room, he gazed at the tile frescoes on the walls. They reminded him of the glory that had once been his.

Here he had reported his diplomatic activities to Nebuchadnezzar. Here he had asked for the hand of the king's beautiful Egyptian daughter, Nitocris.

What happened to her? he wondered. Did they kill her? Or exile her? Will I ever see her again?

And here he had sat upon the divine throne himself, ruling his extensive golden empire.

But now blond, blue-eyed foreigners flanked the walls, and an enemy sat upon the throne. Cyrus the Great ruled Media-Persia, a much larger empire than any that Nebuchadnezzar or his predecessors had governed.

Oh, the humiliation, thought Nabonidus. What a dark night for Babylon and, darkest of all, for me!

Nabonidus came out of his reverie when he heard the soft but authoritative voice of the man who sat on the throne. "Welcome home, Nabonidus," greeted Cyrus. "Welcome into the new world—the world of Media-Persia."

The Babylonian bowed to the floor and remained on his face before Cyrus, but the Persian spoke again. "Arise, Nabonidus." The great king smiled. "Why have you come to see me today?"

Nabonidus got to his feet, squinting at the Persian king in confusion. He'd expected to be seized, bound, and carried off for execution. But Cyrus acted as though he'd come for a friendly chat.

"My l-lord," Nabonidus stammered, and then stopped. He strove to control himself. Straightening his back and squaring his shoulders, he cleared his throat and continued. "I have come to surrender," he said, "for I cannot defeat your over-whelming armies." He paused and gestured toward his com-panions. "You may do with me as you will," he stated, "but I request that you release my men so they may return to their families."

"Your request for the men is granted," replied Cyrus. "I only ask that they surrender their weapons before they leave." He motioned for them to go.

"As for you, Nabonidus," Cyrus continued. "Your kingdom was at an end before I came. The time had come when your people began to rise in revolt against you and your son. They would have eventually killed you themselves, had I not arrived on the scene to protect you."

Nabonidus couldn't believe his ears, but Cyrus gave him all the evidence he needed to convince him. "You canceled Babylon's sacred feasts and forced your nobles to work in labor gangs. Then you left the city in the hands of your un-principled son, who enslaved the people and enriched himself at their expense."

Cyrus watched carefully as Nabonidus's shock grew with each passing revelation. He had been aware of some of his failings, but hearing a recounting of the sum total of his faults almost overwhelmed him.

"Your worst crime," continued Cyrus, "was the slaughter of thousands of innocent Babylonians at Opis." The great king paused, smoothing his royal robes. "Survivors of Opis living in

Babylon have vowed to kill you, Nabonidus." He looked at his fingernails as though he were unconcerned but then leaned forward, staring directly into Nabonidus's eyes. "When I heard of your approach, I commanded my guards to escort you to the palace. Believe me when I say that if I turned you loose in the streets, your own people would tear you to pieces in minutes."

Nabonidus shivered at the thought.

"I will not be as inhuman to you as you have been to others," continued Cyrus. "You performed an invaluable service to Media in former days, and your wife Nitocris has given us important counsel since we have taken the city. If you had followed her suggestions years ago, you might still be sitting on this throne." Cyrus lifted his crown and ran his fingers through his hair. "Nitocris asked us to spare your life, and we have decided to grant her request."

Nitocris! Nabonidus's thoughts played leapfrog in his joy to hear her name. She's still alive—living here in Babylon! He looked around, halfway expecting that she'd be standing on the sidelines, but he didn't see her.

Cyrus cleared his throat before pronouncing sentence upon the royal prisoner. "For your personal safety and as a gesture of goodwill to the honored lady, I hereby exile you to Carmania, to live out your life in isolation. May the gods favor me for the mercy I have extended to my enemies."

Waves of relief swept over Nabonidus as he bowed before the Persian king. "Thank you, my lord." He almost choked on the words. Then he rose to follow his escort—banished from the throne room forever.

In the corridor outside the royal hall, he stopped short, for Nitocris stood before him. She had dressed in sackcloth and sprinkled ashes upon her head—to express her mourning for her son and her husband. She appeared to have aged rapidly. All the stress of the past few months had added years to her body, sapping her of vital strength.

Even so, Nabonidus thought she looked as beautiful as when he'd first laid eyes on her. Oh, how he yearned to take her in his arms, to carry her once more into their chamber . . .

"I'll always love you!" she called as the impatient guards

hustled Nabonidus down the corridor. He looked back over his shoulder and saw his beloved holding out her hands to him, tears streaming down her face. His heart seemed to die inside. He knew he would never see her again.

★　　　　★　　　　★　　　　★

Tens of thousands thronged the courts of Marduk's temple as the group of nobles and royalty ascended the stairs of the famous Tower of Babylon. Not since Nebuchadnezzar's coronation had so many come to witness the inauguration of a new monarch.

This ceremony differed from most, for two kings ascended the heights to receive their crowns. By the decree of Cyrus the Great, king of lands, his son Cambyses would receive the crown as king of Babylonia, ruling the territory once controlled by Nebuchadnezzar and his successors. By a similar decree, Gobryas, governor of Gutium, would receive the crown as king of the city of Babylon—the jewel of the empire.

At the top of the tower, by prearranged plan, two priests administered the royal slap—and tears filled the eyes of both men. The high priest smiled and turned to announce the good news. "Both kings have wept," he called in a loud voice. "Bel will give us a double blessing during the coming year."

The roar of tens of thousands of voices thundered approval as the small group descended to the immense courtyard. Crossing to the temple of Marduk, each royal candidate took hold of the claws of the dragonlike statue. Marduk's stony heart granted each of them divine sanction—and both became elevated to the pantheon of Babylon's god-kings.

The royal party marched in self-composed silence as they returned to the palace. Each man seemed lost in thought as he contemplated the coronation feast to take place later in the evening.

Gobryas broke the silence as the trio reached the place where they would go to their separate quarters. "I plan to change my name," he announced.

"Oh?" grunted Cyrus. "And what do you wish to be called?"

"I've considered this for some time," mused Gobryas. "For

years I've been consumed with the passion to avenge the murder of my son. To me, the name *Gobryas* has become associated with revenge."

"I knew you hated Belshazzar," commented Cyrus. "I felt proud that you handled it the way you did. Others would have killed him on sight."

"That was difficult," admitted Gobryas. "I wanted to tear his heart out with my bare hands, to stamp on his head like he trampled my son to death years ago. But that wouldn't have been right. And no one would have known the extent of his crimes."

"And now you want to put all that behind you?"

"Yes, my lord." Gobryas glanced at the floor for a moment, and then, squaring his shoulders, he looked his noble nephew in the eye. "From hence forth," he announced, "I want to be known as Darius."

"Darius—the Mede," added Cyrus. "Sounds like a good choice."

"Yes, my lord." The new king of Babylon smiled at his master-nephew. "I think it's a fitting name as I begin a new life in a new position."

Cambyses had continued on toward his chambers but returned when he heard the men talking.

"I present to you Darius the Mede," Cyrus declared, bowing and extending his hand toward the new king of Babylon City. "Our uncle desires to start a new life with a new name."

★   ★   ★   ★

Cyrus ascended the steps and seated himself on the throne. He gestured for his son and uncle to occupy the two ornate seats that had been placed for them. The royal chairs rested on a slightly lower level and to either side of the central throne. "Join me, Darius and Cambyses," suggested Cyrus. "Together, we reign as masters of the empire."

"If it please my lords." Darius turned in his seat to address both Cyrus and his son. "In the administration of Babylon, I'd like to retain most of the former officials in their old posts."

"Do you feel you can trust them?" asked Cambyses.

"I've not detected any disloyalty among them," returned Darius. "They know their work, and they do it well. I believe that, with the removal of Belshazzar's corrupt leadership and with proper motivation, they'll do an even better job now than they did in the past."

"I see no reason to disagree with you," replied Cyrus, crossing his legs.

"Nor do I," chimed in Cambyses, shifting his position so as to see his great-uncle better. "It would take many months to train new men to do their work. And think of all the mistakes they'd make while they were learning new jobs."

Cyrus gasped in mock horror. "All those mistakes would make people think we were as bad as Nabonidus!"

They all laughed.

"What will you do with Daniel?" asked Cyrus. "Belshazzar elevated him to—what was it?—third ruler in the kingdom, just before the king was brought to justice."

"I plan to keep him," announced Darius. "I propose to organize all the officials under three presidents, who will report to me. Daniel seems to me the best qualified to act as first president."

"How do we know we can trust him?" Cyrus rose from the throne and descended the stairs. He paced back and forth, head lowered in meditation, hands loosely clasped behind his back. "Everyone knows he was the close friend and confidant of Nebuchadnezzar."

Cyrus stopped and looked at his vassal king, hands now on his hips. "Do you remember when Nebuchadnezzar summoned all his officials to bow before that golden image and declare their loyalty to him?"

"Yes," replied Darius.

"And who was it that refused to bow?"

"Three Jews refused . . ."

"Exactly." Cyrus cut him off. "You know as well as I that if Daniel had been there, he'd have refused to bow too. But he wasn't there. Have you ever wondered why?"

"Yes."

"It's because he was the only man that Nebuchadnezzar

knew to be entirely faithful. He needed no test! And Nebuchadnezzar knew he wouldn't bow, either."

"That sounds like the Daniel I know," replied Darius. "But where was he?"

"I don't know," replied Cyrus. "Nebuchadnezzar sent him on some mission, I suppose, in order to save Daniel's life."

"And it saved Nebuchadnezzar a great deal of embarrassment too," chimed in Cambyses.

A smile came over Darius's face as he remembered the occasion. "It almost saved Nebuchadnezzar from embarrassment." The Gutiumite pointed at Cambyses. "He forgot about Daniel's three friends."

The three kings laughed again.

"But I ask you, Darius," returned Cyrus again. "Can you trust a man who served our enemy so faithfully?"

Darius bowed to Cyrus before he spoke. When he straightened again, his jaw was set, and the tone of his voice earnest. "I believe that Daniel will serve us just as faithfully as he served Nebuchadnezzar," he said. "His religion demands that of him. The only authority he'll favor above his allegiance to us will be his God."

"You think highly of him, don't you?" put in Cambyses.

"Yes, my lord." Darius pounded his fist into his palm. "I'd stake my throne—and my life—on Daniel's loyalty."

"Then you should keep him," replied Cyrus. "And may his God bring blessings to you as well."

Chapter 9
Out of the Lions' Jaws

"You sent for me, my lord?" Daniel bowed, to show his respect for King Darius.

"King Cyrus has issued a decree, and I thought you'd enjoy hearing it before I publish it in Babylon."

"I'm grateful, my lord."

Darius nodded to a nearby scribe. The man cleared his throat, held up a scroll, and began reading in the usual monotone.

"I [am] Cyrus, the king of totality, the great king, the mighty king, the king of Babylon, the king of Sumer and Akkad, the king of the four quarters [of the world].[1] Peace to all the peoples of the empire. I hereby decree that all the gods that Nabonidus carried to Babylon, from whichever cities and nations they came, shall be returned to their own temples. I further decree that all peoples and nations and tongues throughout the empire shall have the right to follow their own customs and worship their own gods without interference from any government or official, whether high or low. Every citizen must obey the laws of his own city and nation, unless they require disobedience of the laws of the Medes and the Persians—that cannot be altered."

"We are blessed to have such an enlightened ruler." Daniel

smiled. "His subjects will serve him gladly."

"My nephew has always felt justice to be imperative," remarked King Darius. "That's why the common people rally to his support wherever he goes."

"No doubt," replied the old Jew.

"I'm pleased with your work, Daniel," the king continued. "You seem to know what's best for the city—much better than the other presidents."

"I'm but an unprofitable servant, my lord." Daniel blushed. "I've merely done my duty."

"You're a most valuable servant to me," countered Darius. "I wish all my staff had your dedication."

"They're all good men, my lord," returned Daniel. He continually sought to find admirable traits in others. "They work as hard as I, and I find them cooperative."

"Of course," apologized Darius. "I had no desire to speak of them in a disparaging way. But you have something special. Your work seems to be blessed by the gods—by your God."

"I serve Him faithfully." Daniel smiled. "And He blesses my work." He rejoiced for the opportunity to witness for his Creator.

"I remember, years ago, when Nebuchadnezzar was king." Darius tilted his head back, his eyes directed toward the ceiling but staring at some distant vision. "Late in his reign—after he appointed me governor of Gutium—he issued a decree praising your God—"

Daniel nodded and smiled, but Darius continued. "If I remember correctly, it went something like this: He 'lives forever. His dominion is an eternal dominion; His kingdom endures from generation to generation. All the peoples of the earth are regarded as nothing. He does as He pleases with the power of heaven and the peoples of the earth. No one can hold back His hand or say to Him: "What have you done?" '[2]"

"Your memory serves you well, my lord," Daniel remarked, surprise lighting up his face.

"How could I ever forget?" returned Darius. "And the decree went on to say, 'I . . . praise and exalt and glorify the King of heaven, because everything He does is right and all His ways

are just. And those who walk in pride He is able to humble."[3]
What a God this Yahweh of yours must be! To humble the
great Nebuchadnezzar—so that he would say—*that!*"

Darius continued to stare into space. He saw in his mind's
eye the form of the greatest king in the world bowing in humble worship of the God of heaven and earth, the God of the
captive Jew who stood before him this very moment. He
looked back at Daniel, studying the wisdom and love that
radiated from his face. What an honor is mine, he thought, to
have such a remarkable man to serve in my court!

Daniel spoke softly. "Our prophet Isaiah compared Yahweh
to the gods of Babylon," he said. "You know how, at the New
Year's festival, the priests tie the images of Bel and Nebo on
the backs of animals and parade them along Procession
Street?"

"Yes, yes," replied Darius. "I've seen it many times."

"Well, Isaiah referred to that in a poem. Listen:

> 'Bel bows down, Nebo stoops.
>   their idols are on beasts and cattle. . . .
>   They stoop, they bow down together. . . .
> Hearken to me, O house of Jacob,
>   all the remnant of the house of Israel,
> who have been borne by me from your birth,
>   carried from the womb;
> even to your old age I am He,
>   and to gray hairs I will carry you.
> I have made, and I will bear;
>   I will carry and will save.'[4]

"Yahweh has no need for animals to bear Him, O king.
Instead, He carries His people and cares for them."

Daniel stopped for a moment, choosing his words carefully.
"If it please the king," Daniel said. "I have a request to bring
before you."

"Say on."

"Nebuchadnezzar brought my people here as captives from
our homeland. He destroyed our cities and our temple—the

temple of the God of heaven and earth. Nebuchadnezzar destroyed it and left it in a heap of ruins."

"How can these things happen to those who worship Yahweh?" Darius seemed perplexed.

"My people forsook Yahweh and worshiped images of metal and stone and wood. For this reason, He was unable to protect us when our enemies came upon us."

"Amazing!"

"But Yahweh promised that one day He would allow us to go back to our land," continued Daniel. "We would rebuild His city and His temple.

"O king, live forever." Daniel's eyes filled with tears. "Make a decree that my people may return to their homeland."

"You've made a reasonable request, Daniel," replied the king. "But I have no authority to make such a decree, for many of your people live outside the city."

"Of course," sighed Daniel.

"Perhaps one day Cyrus will grant your request."

"I pray that he does."

For several minutes Darius sat silently, gazing at the elderly Jew with whom he'd been talking.

"Daniel?" The king leaned forward, his eyes narrowed, his forehead creased. "Will you serve me, even as you served Nebuchadnezzar?"

"Yes, my lord."

"Good." Darius straightened up and motioned to his scribe to record his words. "You, Daniel, will be my first administrator. The other presidents and all the leaders of the city will obey your word. And you will report to me."

He smiled and nodded to the scribe to show that he had finished the message. Turning back to Daniel, he said, "And may the God who has blessed you—and all the kings whom you have served—may He bless me also."

"According to your word, my lord."

"It's the most humiliating thing I've ever experienced," groaned a Persian official to his friends. "The king ignored us!

He gave the highest office in the city to a former slave!"

"Yes," agreed one of his companions. "And to top it all, he's the same man Belshazzar put on top too—next to the king himself." He planted both fists on his hips, anger radiating from every pore of his body. "Darius should have beheaded him, not given him the highest office in the land!"

"You underestimate both the king and Daniel," cautioned a third man. "Daniel was never Babylonian, even though he served his masters well." He looked out the window, his eyes squinting into the setting sun. "He was always devoted to his God over every other authority. That's why he's such a loyal servant."

"Are you on Daniel's side?" sneered the first officer.

"No!" insisted the third, suddenly realizing how patronizing his argument must have sounded to the others. "I'm trying to put the problem into perspective. You'll never solve it unless you study all sides."

"All right." The first man backed off. "It just sounded for a minute like . . ."

"Not at all." The third man frowned. "I want him out of the way as much as you do. I think a Persian, or a Mede—one of us—should have first position. Or someday we'll all kowtow to Daniel's God like Nebuchadnezzar did."

The three men and their servants spied on Daniel, day after day. They searched for something they could construe as a disloyal act against the government. But they couldn't find fault with anything he said or did.

"What can we do?" sighed one of the presidents, slouching onto a bench in the palace garden. "We've probed every part of Daniel's life. I've never seen a more loyal or honest man. He never gets impatient, even with a bungling slave." His voice became strained with exasperation. "He's never dishonest, never shirks his duty. He works longer and harder than anyone else." He shrugged his shoulders. "And yet he never tries to get credit for anything he does, never even asks for a raise in pay!"

"Sound's like you're ready to give him a medal!" growled his friend.

"No, no, no," bristled the first man. "But I'm tired of trying to find fault with him. He's perfect!"

"I'm afraid you're right," returned a third man, shaking his head. "If we ever find any fault, it will be with his worship of that Jewish God of his."

"That's an idea!" interrupted his friend, rising from the bench. "He worships his God as consistently as he does everything else"—he raised his eyebrows and smiled "—and always in the same way."

"You're right," agreed the second man. "He's very predictable, isn't he? Maybe we could set a trap for him."

"What kind of trap?" asked the third, barely able to conceal his excitement.

"Hmmm—how about something like this . . ."

★   ★   ★   ★

Three presidents paraded into the presence of Darius, king of Babylon. Despite the administrators' importance, the chamberlain asked them to stand against the back wall for several minutes while His Majesty concentrated on the audit of a major animal herder. The high officials fidgeted with their robes and frowned at the delay.

"Shuzubu?" asked the king. "Give an accounting of the animals you've kept for the temple offerings and sacrifices."

"My lord." The herdsman bowed and then straightened his shoulders. He stood to his full height, his nose slightly elevated. "I'm proud to say that we've cared for the king's animals in the manner prescribed by the laws of Babylon.

"I was chief herder during the last three years of King Nabonidus," he reported, his high voice winding up to a painful pitch. "And now I've served during the first month of my lord's dominion. In that time we received 7,036 animals to nurture and distribute to the sacred temples throughout the city."

The herdsman paused and referred to a clay tablet on which he'd written his report. "We've disposed of 6,816 large and small cattle,[5] according to our instructions. We still have 220 in our possession, which we plan to distribute during the first part of next week."[6]

"Is this accounting correct?" asked Darius.

"Yes, my lord," replied the palace treasurer. "Shuzubu has given an accurate accounting of his affairs."

"You've done your work well." Darius smiled as he pointed his bejeweled scepter toward the herdsman. "I would that all my officers followed your example."

"Your servant has only done his duty, my lord." The man smiled as he bowed again, turned, and left the throne room.

"Several administrators wish to see you, my lord," bellowed the palace herald. He lifted his ornate, six-foot staff vertically and gave it one quick whack on the throne-room floor. The sharp report triggered a simultaneous blink in every eye.

Darius nodded and extended his royal scepter.

The pompous platoon approached the throne and bowed. "O King Darius, live forever," they recited in unison.

"What is your business?" Darius wondered why the group had come without their leader—Daniel.

The self-appointed spokesman stepped forward to present the petition. "O king, the royal administrators, prefects, satraps, advisers, and governors have all agreed." He exaggerated the list, attempting to make it sound more important. "We believe the king should issue an edict—and enforce the decree—that anyone who prays to any god or man during the next thirty days, except to you, O king, shall be thrown into the lions' den."

The other officials smiled and bowed in unison when their leader mentioned the "lions' den."

The speaker ignored his friends' enthusiasm and continued. "Now, O king, issue the decree and put it in writing so that it cannot be altered—in agreement with the laws of the Medes and Persians, which cannot be annulled."

He handed the king's scribe a scroll on which they had written the decree, and then returned to stand with his cronies.

Darius smiled, heedless of their plot. What a loyal group of officers! he thought. They're afraid that some anti-Persian zealots still hide in the city, and they want to find them. He scrutinized the men for several minutes, mentally analyzing the decree they proposed.

He liked the honor they sought to bestow upon him. No one ask anything of any *god* or man, he thought, for *thirty* days. Any *god*! That's right—I took hold of Marduk's hands—I'm a god now. And thirty days should be long enough. A few days or a week wouldn't suffice. Anyone could cloak his discontent for that long. But thirty days? That ought to be enough time to flush out any traitor.

"You've considered every angle, haven't you?" remarked Darius. He hesitated and glanced back over the decree, underscoring the cuneiform letters with his finger as he silently mouthed the words. Something's not right about this, he thought. It's too well planned.

He repeated the words aloud: ". . . prays to any *god* or man . . . except to King Darius." His smile became a grin as he considered his importance. For another moment he studied the measure while the conspirators maintained their frozen smiles. Suspense mounted, threatening to explode and bring the entire scheme crashing down around their ears.

"All right." The king broke the tension. "Seal it with my ring. Make it law. We'll see if anyone dares disobey my command."

It's the golden image all over again! thought Daniel as he read the king's decree. At eighty-four, he held the highest position in the city—next to Darius himself. Strange, he thought as he reread the document for the third time. This sounds too self-centered for Darius.

However, he had no choice: he must broadcast this strange law even though it could spell his doom. Summoning his personal messenger, he gave him a copy of the document. "This new decree," he said without emotion, "must be announced throughout the city."

As the page took the scroll and left the room, Daniel considered the decree's implications. ". . . anyone who prays to any god or man during the next thirty days, except to King

Darius . . ." He paused. ". . . thrown into the lions' den."

The elder statesman-prophet remembered for a moment the strange vision he'd had some years ago. Four great beasts rose up out of the sea, terrifying and magnificent. He recalled the presence of the angel who had apparently saved his life from those dangerous animals. Could the lions in the Babylonian zoo be more dangerous than those ferocious beasts? He wondered.

The Medes and Persians, for all their good qualities, had developed a monumental pride. They reasoned that their kings had become gods—as with the Babylonians before them. If they were gods, then they could make no mistakes. Therefore, decrees issued by these god-kings became sacred and could never be annulled—not even by the king himself.

Daniel knew all this and realized that the lions'-den law could never be changed. Its drooling jaws had bared its teeth at him and would gape open before him like the tomb seeking to devour him—for the next thirty days.

The blood-red throat of doom projected itself upon the screen of Daniel's daily devotion. The decree forbade him to pray to Yahweh, even in secret! Daniel had not been in the habit of keeping secrets.

Every time he knelt before his window, every time he prayed aloud toward Jerusalem, every time he pleaded with God to open the gates of captivity and let His people go home, he would break the law. And Daniel was not in the practice of breaking laws.

But to keep the law, he reasoned, would break my link with Yahweh. Daniel's stomach churned within him as he shuffled home that night. He felt no hunger gnawing at his innards as on other days. Instead, he sensed an emptiness of spirit.

For a fleeting moment, he remembered others on past occasions who had suffered execution in the lions' den. Shivers rippled up his spine. He felt so alone. Had God forsaken him? No, but his thoughts tumbled over each other as he weighed the alternatives—to pray, or not to pray.

I've always prayed in the morning, he reflected. I've talked with God at noon. I've discussed with Him the events of the day before I slept at night. God is my strength—the lifeblood of my soul. To quit praying, even for thirty days—I'd rather die!

The struggle subsided as quickly as it had appeared. "God has always cared for me," he affirmed aloud. "He's never abandoned me before, and He'll not forsake me now, lions or no lions."

Entering his house, he opened the upstairs window that faced Jerusalem as he had done hundreds of times. Kneeling there with outstretched arms, he poured out his heart to God.

"O Yahweh, Creator of heaven and earth," he prayed. "Thank You for creating me and for sustaining me through all these years. Thank You for giving me opportunity to show Your greatness to those in high places, even to the kings of Babylon and Media-Persia.

"Now, O Yahweh, You've seen the decree published by King Darius today. You see how this man—or could it be his advisors? . . . You see how this decree robs Your people of the privilege of calling upon You day and night. Mortal man has thought to take for himself the glory that belongs only to You."

The prophet paused as he thought about the decree. "I pray that You will overrule, that You will humble those who seek to take Your place, and glorify Your name before the heathen."

Tears ran down his cheeks as he continued. "Give me wisdom, O God, that I may lead the king to know You, so that he may serve You and love You even as I do this day."

As Daniel closed his prayer, his mind filled with a psalm he had known since childhood, and he began to recite it aloud:

> "God is our refuge and strength,
>   an ever present help in trouble.
> Therefore we will not fear, though the earth give way
>   and the mountains fall into the heart of the sea,
>   though its waters roar and foam
>   and the mountains quake with their surging."[7]

Rising from his knees, Daniel glanced out the window. Strange, he thought. Several city officers are watching me. I've never seen them do that before.

He felt much better now that he'd laid his burden upon the

Creator, and he turned to his evening meal.

"My lord," Daniel's servant pleaded. "The king's decree! You should be more careful."

"Yes, my friend," Daniel replied.

"But why don't you pray in your closet?" the man insisted. "You know how much the others want to get rid of you."

Daniel put his hand on the servant's shoulder. "It makes no matter who wants to hurt me or what decree they issue," he explained. "No earthly power has the right to come between me and my God."

He thought no more about those who'd watched him pray until he knelt before the window again the following morning. As he finished his prayer he heard a stir in the hedgerow at the end of the house. Glancing in that direction, he again saw several city officers observing his behavior—the same men who'd watched him last night.

It's a trap, he thought, smiling. They've caught me in the act of breaking the new decree. "Well, Yahweh," he prayed out loud, "I guess I'll soon become acquainted with some of Your four-footed creatures."

Strange, he thought. I don't feel afraid anymore. What did Isaiah say? "Thou wilt keep him in perfect peace, whose mind is stayed on thee: because he trusteth in thee."[8]

"Yahweh," he continued his prayer. "You made the lions, and You can control them. If You're finished with me, and the lions need my flesh to sustain them, may Your will be done. But," he persisted, "if You have more work for me to do, then I know You can save me—even from the lions' jaws."

"O king, live forever."

Darius hadn't expected to see his administrators and their friends again so soon. He'd granted their request just yesterday; what more could they want?

The men bowed before the king, and their leader scrambled forward, beginning to chatter without even receiving the king's permission to speak. "Did you not publish a decree," he declared, "that during the next thirty days anyone who prays to any god or man except to you, O king, would be thrown into the lions' den?"

Are they questioning my sanity? wondered Darius. "The decree stands—in agreement with the laws of the Medes and the Persians," he snapped, irritated by their lack of courtesy. "It cannot be annulled." He hardly thought he'd need to remind them, since they'd made such a point of it yesterday.

The group of men snickered as their leader dropped his bombshell: "With all due respect, my lord, Daniel, who is one of the exiles from Judah, pays no attention to you, O king, or to the decree you put in writing. He still prays three times a day to his god."

What! thought Darius. Daniel *still* prays! Anger welled up within his mind at the idea that his highest official disobeyed the law. But the indignation quickly melted as he thought about the man he'd come to know.

Of course, he reasoned. Daniel *always* prays. These presidents knew that too! The king's facial expression passed quickly from surprise to bewilderment to rage within seconds.

"So!" he thundered. "This whole charade of loyalty to me was only a ploy to destroy Daniel!"

Darius had been aware of the friction these administrators felt against Daniel, but he hadn't realized its lethal magnitude. He couldn't believe that these men would seek to kill the greatest man in the empire.

The knife of guilt pierced the king's heart. His conscience goaded him as he realized that he had stooped to aid these scoundrels—however unwittingly. How could I have been so blind? he chastened himself. Why didn't I see through their murderous scheme? "Oh Yahweh," he pleaded to Daniel's God. "I've sinned. Help me!"

He turned on the conspirators. "Daniel is the most trusted man in the kingdom," he objected. "The law was never meant to . . ."

"But my lord," interrupted the leader, now displaying a mock courtesy he had ignored before. "Your decree says 'anyone.' And the laws of the Medes and the Persians . . ."

"Cannot be changed." The king's voice wore a razor edge as

he finished the leader's sentence. "I know the law! Get out of here!" he shouted. "You've laid a scheme to murder the most loyal man in the kingdom. I'll not let you do it!"

The men bowed and turned to leave. "But my lord," the leader's voice carried a menacing threat. "The law cannot be changed. If you don't throw Daniel into the lions' den by sunset tonight, the judges will want to know why."

Darius's heart felt sick. He liked Daniel. He trusted him more than any other person in the city. Daniel's life, his fidelity, his courtesy, his love for all living beings. Darius wished he could be like that—so dedicated to the One who had created all things.

But he'd painted himself into a corner. He couldn't see any escape. Arising from his throne, he left the hall without a word.

"Others await an audience," called the herald to the retreating king. "Will you return . . . ?"

Darius disappeared into an antechamber without answering. The herald shrugged his shoulders. "The king has recessed for the day," he announced. "If you must see him, you will have to return tomorrow."

The disgruntled people who waited to see the king called to the palace officer, each explaining why their case had such importance that it must be heard today. The herald ignored them and shut the door, leaving them all complaining among themselves.

Darius wanted to be alone. "There must be some way . . ." he mumbled aloud. But even as the words escaped his lips, he knew it was hopeless. Yet he studied his law books for hours, seeking an answer from reason, examining the case from every angle.

Calling in his legal scribe, he explained the predicament, pleading for counsel on how to change a legal decree.

"My lord," replied the scribe, sympathetic to the king's cause, "there is no way to change your decree." He bowed again to Darius and showed how steeped he had become in Persian culture. "But why would you want to change your decree? You're a god. You don't make mistakes. This man Daniel may seem to be good, but if he broke a Persian law, he must be a very bad man."

Darius felt irritated by the reply of this naïve palace servant. "It wasn't the god in me that did this," he answered, exasperated. "The *man* in me made this decree. I've got to find some way to change it, or I'll have to execute my best friend."

"I'm sorry, my lord." The scribe began to sense how deeply the king felt about this matter. "But the laws of the Medes and the Persians leave no room for human error. We cannot change a king's decree."

Toward evening a palace guard interrupted Darius. "My lord," he announced, "a group of high officials wish to speak with you."

"Tell them to go away," snapped the king. "I'll see them tomorrow."

The guard disappeared for a minute, but returned. "I'm sorry, my lord. They won't go. They insist on seeing you now."

"Oh, all right," he barked. "But tell them to make it short."

The presidents and their cronies shuffled into the king's chamber. "What do you want?" hissed Darius.

The leader displayed surprise at the king's anger but recovered instantly. "Remember, O king," he recited in his practiced voice. "The laws, decrees, and edicts of the Medes and the Persians cannot be changed."

"I know! I know!" bellowed Darius.

"We, the leading judges of Babylon," the leader continued, "demand that you carry out the law. We witnessed the crime, and we insist that the king execute the guilty party."

"But I can't kill Daniel." The king's voice had turned into pleading. "He's the most loyal man I have. He's my friend."

The leader's face reddened in anger, but he managed to control his voice. "The decree demands that you throw Daniel to the lions, my lord. We intend to assure that the *king* obeys the decree."

Darius appeared to melt before them. He'd tried to find some way to get around the law, but he could discover no loophole that would permit him to save his friend. He had no other choice.

"Bring Daniel here," he muttered to the guard. The soldier

and the accused returned within minutes.

"Why haven't you chained the prisoner?" the leader scolded the guard when he ushered Daniel into their presence.

Darius held up his hand. "You've won your wish to destroy the wisest man in Babylon," he hissed, "but I'll not let you humiliate him."

"All right, my lord," conceded the leader as the group left for the royal zoo, "you're the king. Just see that he doesn't escape."

The royal troupe arrived at the lions' pit in the gathering twilight. They stood around the small entrance that opened into a large round hole in the ground. The zookeepers had already slid a sizable flat stone over the opening for the night. From time to time, in the past, they'd tossed food to the beasts through the hole, but they hadn't fed the animals for several days.

"Throw him in!" demanded the leader of the opposition as the guards removed the stone to expose the open pit. "Feed him to the lions!"

Darius had to raise his voice in order to be heard over the roaring of the hungry beasts. "The law requires that we put him into the den," he agreed, glaring at Daniel's enemies. "But he's eighty-four years old. The fall could kill him, even if the lions don't." He turned to a guard and spoke in a kinder voice: "Fetch a length of cord and some rags. We don't want the ropes to burn him."

The guard obeyed, though he couldn't understand why the king would take such precautions. "Everybody knows," he told his companions, "that the lions will kill him right away. Seems to me, it'd be more merciful if he died in the fall."

"Don't fear, O king," encouraged Daniel. "Our Scriptures promise that God will protect us when we serve Him faithfully." He put his hand on the king's drooping shoulders. "One of our prophets—Isaiah—wrote:

'Do not fear, for I am with you;
　do not be dismayed, for I am your God.
I will strengthen you and help you;

I will uphold you with my righteous right hand.' "[9]

"Thank you, Daniel." Darius could hardly speak. "May your God, whom you serve continually, rescue you!"

Slowly they lowered the old man into the hole. The guards grimaced at the sound of the lions' roars, bracing themselves so that the creatures' attack on Daniel wouldn't pull them into the pit with him. Strange, they thought as Daniel neared the bottom. The lions should have attacked him by now.

But they didn't attack. Once Daniel reached the floor of the den, he untied the ropes and waved at the king. The guards began to move the stone over the opening, and the light faded fast. The old man glanced around the cave. Several grown lions stared at him, breathing heavily and growling. But they made no move to attack.

In the corner of the den he found a clear area and some straw. He sat down. Nothing changed. He felt weary from the stress of the day, so he lay down on the straw and closed his eyes. He heard the low regular breathing of an animal nearby.

Daniel's sleepy mind reached out to God in prayer, but he had difficulty concentrating. The words of a psalm he'd learned in boyhood drifted through his mind:

> "This poor man called, and the Lord heard him;
>   he saved him out of all his troubles.
> The angel of the Lord encamps around those who fear him,
>   and he delivers them."[10]

"Thank you, Yahweh," he breathed as he drifted into untroubled sleep.

Daniel opened his eyes and peered around the darkened enclosure. It took him a moment to realize he wasn't in his bedroom at home. But the floor felt cold and hard, and the acrid smell of animal sewage flooded his nostrils. Moonlight streamed through a tiny crack above, between the edge of the hole and its rock lid.

Across the cave, he counted three male lions and thirteen females. Some slept, while others paced around the floor. Occasionally they grumbled among themselves, quarreling like their miniature tabby cousins but creating a lot more noise.

Only then did he make out the form of an enormous male lying at his side. The huge head swung around to face him, and he saw no fear or malice in the animal's great golden eyes. Without thinking, he patted the monster on his flank. The lion's flesh quivered at his touch, and he began to lick Daniel's leg, as one feline would groom another. Somehow, the prophet felt secure with this beast at his side.

Daniel pulled his cloak about him to ward off the chilled night air. The lion stopped licking his leg and turned to watch the others, who'd become restless. The vibrations of their roaring ricocheted about the cave, nearly deafening the old man. The presence of "food" within their reach seemed to increase their ravenous appetites.

The pride across the room began to pace in an interweaving pattern, studying Daniel and drooling as though they'd already tasted his blood. They maneuvered into an instinctive hunting arrangement, crouching, stalking, ready to pounce at any moment.

The prophet sat quietly, stroking the giant beast at his side. No fear quickened his heart; no adrenalin flowed through his veins; only peace prevailed in his soul. He'd surrendered his life to God—to live or to die according to His will.

The pride prepared to attack, inching into position, muscles stretched like rubber bands. But they suddenly backed away, pawing their noses like naughty boys hiding their faces when caught in forbidden mischief. The huge lion had risen and now stood before the prophet, glaring at the others as if to say, "This one is mine."

Daniel lay down again, drifting off into a childlike sleep.

★   ★   ★   ★

At the first light of dawn, the king hastened to the den. "Open the cave," he barked to his guards. "Hurry!"

The men bent to the task while Darius fidgeted with his

staff. "Is he still alive?" he asked no one in particular. "Has his God saved him?"

The workers looked askance at their king. Had he lost his mind? "No one could survive a night in the lions' den," they assured him.

Darius paid them no attention as he paced about. The opening began to widen as the stone lumbered aside on its rollers. He got down on his knees and peered into the gap. "It's so dark down there," he complained. "I can't see the bottom."

"Daniel," he called, impatient to know the truth. "Daniel, servant of the living God! Has your God, whom you serve continually, been able to rescue you from the lions?"

The guards smiled at one another. This is stupid, they thought. The king is talking to bones!

But Darius knew Daniel—and he'd begun to know Daniel's God. His faith clung to a thin thread of hope that maybe . . .

The stone had cleared the opening now, and Darius heard what sounded like a yawn. Could it be human? The king knelt in the dust, peering into the abyss. "Daniel! Are you all right?"

"O king, live forever!" The voice from the lions' den sounded strong and full of life. "My God sent His angel, and he shut the mouths of the lions."

Darius's eyes had become accustomed to the dim light, and he could see Daniel standing on the floor of the den.

"The lions haven't hurt me," the old man said, "because I was found innocent in God's sight." He paused, studying the face of his friend, framed by the entrance of the den above him. "Nor have I ever done any wrong before you, O king."

Darius glanced at his open-mouthed guards. "Get him out of there," he barked. Tears streamed down the royal face as he contemplated the gentle rebuke of this man of God.

Oh, the shame, his mind chastised him. I fell into the trap of evil men and—but for a miracle of God—almost killed my best friend. "O Yahweh!" The cry erupted from his broken heart. "Don't let me ever make a mistake like this again!"

The presidents and their fellow schemers trotted up to the den and quickly realized what had happened. "He's still alive?" gasped the leader, fear and confusion distorting his face.

"Yes," bellowed the king. "No thanks to you."

"Put the loop under your arms," called the guard as he tossed a coil of rope into the pit. "Hang on tight. Be careful not to swing against the wall."

Daniel's enemies cursed their gods as the guards slowly drew the old prophet from the deep pit. They stomped around, hands on hips, shouting accusations at each other and accusing Daniel of trickery to escape punishment for his crimes.

Daniel braced his feet against the wall as he neared the opening of the pit. Already the lions complained loudly that their "meal" had been taken away.

As the guards removed the ropes, Daniel wiped his eyes and adjusted them to the light of the rising sun. "My lord!" he cried, recognizing Darius and bowing to show his respect.

Darius had him rise. "Are you all right, Daniel?" he asked. "Have you been hurt?"

"Yes, my lord." Daniel smiled. "I'm all right. The lions didn't hurt me at all. The large male kept the others from hurting me."

"Large male?" asked the lion keeper in alarm. "There's no large ma—"

"It's all a trick," objected the leader of the opposition. "Daniel must have fed the lions before you put him into the pit. I'd bet my life on it."

"You would?" The king raised his eyebrows and glared at the president.

The schemer froze. "I-I-It's just a manner of s-s-speaking, m-my lord," he stammered, terror etched on his face. "I-I didn't mean . . ."

"Guards!" The king cut him off. "Let's test this man's theory. Put him and his cronies—and their families—down into the pit." He turned to look at the trembling man. "Well, my brave fellow, what's the matter with you? If Daniel fed them so well that he could spend an entire night with them, unharmed, you haven't a thing to worry about."

"Don't do it, my lord!" Daniel cried. "They won't have a chance down there." No matter that they had tried to kill him. Daniel did his best to save their lives.

King Darius held up his hand. "I know your love for others, Daniel, even for your enemies. But doesn't your own law demand that a false witness receive the punishment he desired to give the accused?[11] Our laws demand the same. It's only justice."

"But their families?" objected Daniel. "Why punish them too?"

Darius put his hand on Daniel's shoulder. "You know as well as I do that these men hatched their foul scheme at home. Their families helped them plan the entire intrigue. They're just as guilty as the ones who carried out the crime."[12]

Daniel's elation over God's act of protecting him from a night in the lions' pit wilted into grief as he contemplated the punishment of his accusers.

"You needn't stay," consoled the king. "Go home now. Get some rest."

As Darius watched to assure that his sentence would be put into effect, Daniel turned toward home. The prophet felt sick. When he'd prayed for God's enemies to be humbled, he had no idea the curse would strike so close to home.

When the elder statesman had turned the corner and disappeared from view, the king nodded for the guards to begin. They grasped one of the presidents by his arms, holding him fast as he screamed and tried to wriggle free. They tied a rope around his chest and wrestled him over the opening. He fought them, grasping the edges, first with his feet and then with his hands, trying to prevent their lowering him into the pit. But the guards overcame him. As they lowered him—in spite of his wild cries—the lions roared ferociously.

"Pull me up!" he cried. "Pull me u—" All human sound suddenly ended when the rope went slack. The guards glanced into the pit, but grimaced and quickly turned away. The roaring of the lions became deafening.

One by one, the guards continued their grizzly job. They lowered the other men, and then rounded up their wives and children, each to suffer an equal fate. None of the condemned lived long enough to stand on the floor of the lions' den. And the beasts filled themselves with their flesh.

★   ★   ★   ★

"How could you be so calm when we put you into the lions' den?" asked Darius. "They might have eaten you."

"I knew God was with me," explained Daniel. "If He had more work for me to do, He'd save me from the lions. If He had no more work for me—well—in either case, He was with me, and that's what counted."

"I'm thankful it came out the way it did."

"I am too," replied Daniel. "The evil one tried to destroy me and my opportunity to share God's truth with others."

"The evil one?" Darius wrinkled his forehead.

"The great enemy of God," answered Daniel. "He once held the highest position in heaven, like the three presidents who died today."

"Ah, yes." Darius smiled. "But he'll not prevail."

"No. Lucifer—that's his name—tried to overthrow God, to throw Him to the lions, as it were. But Isaiah says God will destroy him."[13]

"Like I did with those rogues who tried to kill you?"

"Yes," answered Daniel. "And when God destroys him, everyone will be satisfied with God's justice."

★   ★   ★   ★

"Then King Darius wrote to all the peoples, nations and men of every language throughout the land: 'May you prosper greatly! I issue a decree that in every part of my kingdom people must fear and reverence the God of Daniel. For he is the living God and he endures forever; his kingdom will not be destroyed, his dominion will never end. He rescues and he saves; he performs signs and wonders in the heavens and on the earth. He has rescued Daniel from the power of the lions.' "[14]

---

1. Cyrus's title as it appears in an inscription, recorded in the book *Nabonidus and Belshazzar: A study of the closing events of the Neo-Babylonian Empire*, by Raymond Philip Dougherty (New Haven: Yale University Press, 1929), p. 177.

2. Daniel 4:34, 35.

3. Daniel 4:37.

4. Isaiah 46:1-4, RSV.

5. Large and small cattle: an ancient expression referring to cattle and sheep/goats.

6. An actual audit reported by William H. Shea in his article, "A Vassal King of Babylon," *Andrews University Seminary Studies*, vol. 10, no. 2, July 1971, p. 118.

7. Psalm 46:1-3.

8. Isaiah 26:3, KJV.

9. Isaiah 41:10.

10. Psalm 34:6, 7.

11. See Deuteronomy 19:18, 19.

12. Ancient customs took for granted that the closeness of the family implied that wives and children all helped in the evil plans and were therefore as guilty as the father. Compare Leviticus 20:4, 5. Another example is found in Esther 5:9-14; 6:12-14, where Haman and his wife plotted together the destruction of the Jews.

13. Isaiah 14:12-19; Ezekiel 28:12-19.

14. Daniel 6:25-27.

Chapter 10

Open the Gates

"The king is dead," wailed the palace herald, his voice breaking at intervals. "May the king live forever."

Darius had served in several high positions. Nebuchadnezzar regarded him as one of his favored generals and later appointed him governor of Gutium. Under Cyrus he conquered Babylon and reigned as its first Media-Persian king.

But now his body lay embalmed—displayed in the first courtyard of the old palace. The royal morticians had dressed him in his favorite robes and arranged for elite Median guardsmen to act as honor sentries. In this way, King Darius made his last public appearance.

The most important people in his life grouped around the bier. They had dressed in sackcloth, with ashes sprinkled on their heads. Among them, cross-legged on the pavement, sat Nitocris—daughter of Nebuchadnezzar and wife of former King Nabonidus. Darius had allowed her to stay in the palace and considered the woman one of his trusted counselors.

Nearby sat an aging Jewish prophet, dressed in similar attire. He loved the Median king and wept at his death. "A sincere man," he remarked to Nitocris. "He learned to serve Yahweh, just like your father."

The former Babylonian queen smiled. She liked the gentle

Jew. She had secretly worshiped his God after her father had been converted.

"Darius was a good man," she told Daniel, tears gathering on her lower eyelids. "His justice was painful, though. It cost me my husband and my son. But I admired him for insisting on righting all wrongs."

Thousands of people filed by the bier for a last look at the man who'd conquered them—and saved them from tyranny. In less than a year he'd won their hearts, and many expressed genuine grief.

Daniel glanced at Nitocris. She looks so tired, he mused. She's six years older than Darius, and she's had a hard existence for a queen. And yet, she's had a full life.

The old prophet mentally reviewed the effect she'd had on the kingdom. Her influence held the empire together during the madness of Belshazzar's reign, he thought. Few realized how much they owed to her.

The city still mourned its fallen Median king when—just sixteen days later—Nitocris closed her eyes for the last time. The daughter of Nebuchadnezzar had become a legend during her own lifetime. She represented Babylon's last royal tie with the greatness of Chaldea's golden days. The people lamented her death more than they had grieved for Darius.

Six weeks lumbered by after the passing of Darius. The official mourning ended, and everyone returned to their work. The nobles and priests didn't replace Darius with another king for fear they'd get in trouble with Cyrus, who now resided at his palace in Susa.

One morning a trumpet blast sounded from the outer gate, far to the north of the old city. Though the sound was faint to those within the ancient walls, many heard it and paused to listen. The lively cadence floated through the hot midday air, and other signalmen picked up the tune, echoing the strain all around the city.

A royal herald pounded through the gates and urged his stallion up and down the streets: "The king is coming!" he shouted. "The king is coming! Cyrus the Great, king of lands, is coming to Babylon! Come out to meet him!"

The watchmen atop the Ishtar Gate observed the royal troop approaching and added their trumpet call to the signal already wafting around the city. Cyrus rode astride his favorite white horse, flanked by guards, pages, and servants. A small army followed closely behind, but no one doubted that the bulk of his troops had encamped nearby, awaiting his command.

As Cyrus advanced through the gates, crowds of people waved their hands and scarves and palm plumes to their supreme monarch. After the tense weeks without a king to settle noble disputes, they rejoiced over the presence of one who had authority.

When the king dismounted before the palace gate, those nearest him observed that he wore sackcloth beneath his outer cloak. No crown or any other kind of covering graced his head. A trace of ashes speckled his blond hair.

Cyrus approached the stone monument that marked the spot where the bier had rested and bowed his head in Darius's honor. Those approved because of their rank or position followed him, removing their head coverings as they entered the courtyard.

"Gobryas—my beloved uncle," he murmured. "You were the one who gave the kingdom to me." A tear trickled down his cheek as he sank to the ground, crossed his legs, and began to rock back and forth in his grief. His servants followed his example.

After many minutes, the king arose and looked at those who stood around him. He saw Daniel standing in the corner of the courtyard, his head lowered in meditation. Without a word, Cyrus moved toward the old Jew as the multitude parted to allow him room. Daniel looked up just as the great king approached.

Cyrus spoke quietly. "Daniel," he said, "my uncle wrote me of the assistance you've given him." He paused, studying the tranquil face and kind eyes of the elder statesman. "I'll need your counsel, too, now more than ever."

★   ★   ★   ★

"Seventy years." Daniel sat at a table in his library reading from the writings of Jeremiah. "God promised that His people could return to Judah in seventy years.[1] Then why . . . ?" The aging prophet retrieved another scroll from the shelf and unrolled it beside Jeremiah's.

The newer scroll, written by Daniel himself, described a vision given him ten years previously. He scanned over the columns, searching them for the dozenth time, looking to see if he could harmonize his vision with Jeremiah's older prophecy.

"Here," he muttered, pointing his finger to well-worn words. "He said to me, 'Unto two thousand and three hundred days; then shall the sanctuary be cleansed.'[2] But how does that mesh with Jeremiah's seventy years?" His eyes followed his finger down the page. "Ah." He smiled. " 'The vision of the evenings and mornings that has been given you is true, but seal up the vision, for it concerns the distant future.' "[3] He touched his lips and thought again. "Perhaps these two time periods speak of different events."

The prophet mulled the message over in his mind, reading and rereading the Jeremiah passage. He wrote several numbers on scraps of papyrus that lay at his elbow and added the column. The sum equaled seventy. He'd done the simple math exercise many times before, always with the same result.

"It's time!" he shouted, pounding his fist on the table.

"Time for what?" Daniel's servant looked in at the open door.

"Time for the Jews to go home," answered the prophet. "Time for them to rebuild their city and Yahweh's temple."

A light seemed to flash in Daniel's eyes as he once more retrieved a scroll from the shelves. For several minutes he rolled material from one spindle to another, scanning the text as it passed his view. His lips mouthed the words he sought, but he made no audible sound.

"There!" He stabbed his finger at the Hebrew characters and smiled. "Listen to this." He beckoned to his servant.

The quiet, efficient attendant had often come to his master's study. Even though the wise man was well into his nineties, he had enthusiasm and physical strength exceeding many younger men. He's so different from others, thought the aide. I'm glad I work for Daniel—and know about his God.

The old Jew read from the ancient scroll: " 'I will raise up Cyrus in my righteousness: I will make all his ways straight. He will rebuild my city and set my exiles free.'[4]

"That, my friend," Daniel tapped his finger to the cadence of his words, "was written 210 years ago."

★   ★   ★   ★

Daniel smiled at the doorkeeper as he entered the throne room. He carried an old leather scroll under his right arm. "May the king live forever," he stated as he bowed before Cyrus.

The Persian beamed: "And to what do I owe the honor of your visit, O wise and righteous president?" For some reason, whenever Daniel appeared, Cyrus felt that the atmosphere seemed sweeter and his heart lighter.

Daniel glowed as he took the double scroll from under his arm. "I've discovered a passage in an ancient Hebrew book that I thought might interest you."

"Ancient Hebrew?" Cyrus wrinkled his forehead in concentration. "I'm always intrigued by the wisdom of the ancients. Come up here and show me."

Daniel climbed the steps and laid the scroll gently on the king's lap. Cyrus didn't understand Hebrew, but he seemed fascinated by the strange letters.

Daniel told Cyrus some of the background of the book. "The Jewish prophet Isaiah wrote this in the days of Hezekiah, king of Judah, and Sennacherib, king of Assyria."

The Persian made some mental calculations and let out a low whistle. "Why, that's—that's about 200 years ago." His awe at the age of the scroll caused him to speak in a whisper.

"Two hundred and ten years, to be exact," replied Daniel. "Now, listen to what he wrote: 'This is what the Lord says— your Redeemer, . . . who has made all things . . . who says to the watery deep, "Be dry, and I will dry up your streams," who says of Cyrus,—' "

The Persian felt a jolt pass through his body at the mention of his name. "What did it say about streams?" he asked, excitedly.

Daniel repeated the passage.

"That's what my army did—what Uncle Gobryas did to the Euphrates River when he conquered Babylon!"

Daniel continued to read, tracing the words with his finger so the king could follow. " 'Who says of Cyrus, "He is my shepherd and will accomplish all that I please; he will say of Jerusalem, 'Let it be rebuilt,' and of the temple, 'Let its foundations be laid.' " This is what the Lord says to his anointed, to Cyrus, whose right hand I take hold of to subdue nations before him and to strip kings of their armor, to open doors before him so that gates will not be shut: I will go before you and will level the mountains; I will break down gates of bronze and cut through bars of iron." " 'I will raise up Cyrus in my righteousness: I will make all his ways straight. He will rebuild my city and set my exiles free, . . . says the Lord Almighty.' "[5]

Cyrus stared at the manuscript on his lap, unable to comprehend at once what Daniel had read. "You mean—Yahweh subdued all those nations before me? He caused the gates of Babylon to be open for me—for Gobryas? So I could serve Him?"

"Yes, my lord." Daniel stepped back. "Yahweh, the God who made heaven and earth, gave you victory over all your enemies. He made all nations serve you, from the east to the west. He raised you up for a special purpose—to send His people back to their homeland."

Daniel looked down at the scroll for a moment and then back at the king. "God gave you more authority and power than any king before you—even greater than Nebuchadnezzar. He did this so you would do His will. He wants you to open the gates of slavery and let His people go. O king," Daniel pleaded, "fulfill God's purpose for you. Release the Jews from bondage, and let them return to their own land. Let them rebuild their city, restore their temple, and once again serve Yahweh, their God."

Cyrus stared at Daniel. His mouth opened to speak, but no words came. He gazed at the scroll still lying on his lap and fingered the yellowed leather parchment. The Hebrew characters seemed to run together into rows of inkblots and dance around on the page. He tried to focus, but he couldn't.

Daniel stood before the king, praying silently that God would impress this heathen monarch with the importance of his request. Seconds ticked into minutes; the hall became so quiet that the prophet heard his own heart beating.

Cyrus seemed confused, looking first at the scroll and then at Daniel, unsure what to do next. At length he found his voice. "I-I-I need to th-think about this," he stammered as he rerolled the scroll and handed it back to the old statesman. "S-such an honor!"

Daniel bowed and turned to leave, but Cyrus called him back.

"Thank you for showing me the scroll." He paused, his face reflecting an inner anxiety. "Pray to your God for me," he begged. "Perhaps He'll bless me—" He almost felt blasphemous for thinking such thoughts, but they'd already escaped his lips—"with a portion of the spirit He's given you."

Cyrus felt awed by the soft glow that appeared to surround him. In his mind, it seemed as though a sweet, melodious voice whispered in his ear: "Open the gates. Let My people go."

For a moment, his heart filled with peace. He sensed the presence of a mighty being, yet he had no fear. Instead, all the happiness of a lifetime flooded over his soul. He'd heard no voice. But the message came through clearly, and he wanted to obey. He had an intense desire to open the gates, to let God's people return to their homeland.

It must be Yahweh—Daniel's God, he thought, still overwhelmed by the experience. Everything about Him agrees with what I've seen in Daniel.

"I'll do it," Cyrus whispered, still astonished by the presence. "I'll make a decree—let the Jewish captives go home—

rebuild their city—their temple. I'll . . ."

His reverie died when his chamberlain stomped into the room.

"My lord." The official frowned. "There's been trouble at the Jewish colony again."

"Oh?" The light disappeared, and Cyrus fought to regroup his thoughts.

"Yes, my lord." The chamberlain showed his irritation. "A young Jew assaulted a home guard and almost killed him."

All the king's joy evaporated.

"What!" he shouted. "Trouble with the Jews again?"

Darkness gathered. Anger swept with hurricane fury though the Persian's mind, blasting away every vestige of peace. His heartbeat quickened. Pearls of perspiration appeared on his brow. His muscles tensed. He clenched his fists and his teeth.

"Bring that Jew-swine to me!" he roared. "I'll teach those treacherous Hebrews to rebel against Cyrus the Great!"

Justice descended swiftly and brutally. And the grizzly execution effectively quenched all patriotism from the over-zealous heart of the young, impatient Jew.

Cyrus returned from the slaying confused. "That pig deserved to die," he mumbled. "Let it be a lesson to all who desire to resist my rule."

He sat down to rest on a bench overlooking the palace garden. The scene reminded him of a story Nitocris had told him during his brief stay after the conquest: Nebuchadnezzar became mad and ate grass in this garden. When he regained his sanity, he became a worshiper of Yahweh, God of the Jews.

"The Jews!" He shook his head. "What a mixed bag of fruit they've turned out to be! Some good—some bad." The fury of the past hour drained from his heart as he recalled the scroll and the faithful work of . . .

"Daniel." He smiled. "What a man! I wish I had more like him."

The garden lightened, and the presence returned. "Open the gates. Let My people go."

The presence and the peace seemed so foreign, so contrary

to the anger and retaliation that had controlled him during the past hour.

What's happening to me? he wondered. Am I going mad like Nebuchadnezzar?

The peace felt good but so alien.

Terror seized him. "Who is it?" he shouted, looking around. "What do you want from me?"

A personal servant ran to his side, startled by the king's outcry. "You called for me, my lord?"

"No!" roared Cyrus, suddenly overwhelmed with rage. "How dare you enter my presence without a summons!"

The man scurried backward out of sight, bowing half a dozen times as he went.

"Let the Jews go?" Cyrus bellowed to no one in particular. "Why should I do that? It would upset the economy if all those people left at once."

He dismissed the idea and returned to the throne room. I'll busy myself with settling disputes between wealthy nobles, he reasoned. That ought to bring me out of this nightmare.

It didn't work. Even in the throne room—surrounded by guards and nobles and pages and servants, listening to complaints, and making statements of judgment—the presence remained. And the message persisted to resound within his brain: "Open the gates—open the gates. Let My people go."

Cyrus continued to resist. Day after day he immersed himself in the affairs of state. But he couldn't shake the voice!

He played war games with his guards, honed his swordsmanship, improved his riding skills. The presence remained. He couldn't sleep at night. The room appeared to be filled with light and with that promise of peace! But I don't want peace! his mind screamed. Peace would bring an end to all war and strife. Then there'd be no more need for kings like me!

But wait a bit. The sandals of his mind dragged in the dirt as he tried to stop his thoughts. That's what I've been fighting for—to end all war. He sat up in bed, running his hands through his hair. What's wrong with me?

He scolded his servants, nagged his officials, berated his friends. His judgments at court became tyrannical. Many who sought royal settlements decided to wait for a more favorable time.

"I've faced immense armies," he shouted in his bedchamber one day. "I've struggled with enemies hand to hand—fighting for my very life!"

He pulled at his hair. Sweat poured from his brow, trickling into his beard. Nothing had ever torn his soul like this, this presence, this command to allow a few thousand Jews to go back home.

A week passed, then two weeks. No letup.

Cyrus imagined that the Isaiah scroll floated up before him, and he thought he heard the old prophet's voice again, reading: "I will raise up Cyrus in my righteousness: I will make all his ways straight . . . I will dry up your streams . . . Gates will not be shut. . . . He will rebuild my city and set my exiles free. . ."

"How could an ancient prophet know my name?" he yelled.

Palace guards charged into his chamber, swords at ready, assuming an assassin had attacked their master. They withdrew in confusion when they realized that no visible enemy threatened his life.

Cyrus held his head in his hands, moaning: "How could someone living 210 years ago know how my armies would conquer Babylon? I don't understand. And how would he know I'd send the Jews back to Judah? I haven't done that! I don't want to do that! And yet—" he shook his head. "Yet the ancient scroll says that's what I'm going to do."

Cyrus refused to leave his bedchamber. He paced the floor hour after hour. He stopped at times to sip wine from a silver goblet that sat on a table beside his bed or to nibble goat cheese or barley cakes. He felt like some monstrous force was tearing him in half—pulling him this way and that. His mind approached the breaking point.

Sweat poured from his body. His hands shook. His eyes were puffy, showing strain from days of tension and nights without sleep.

"The presence tells me," he moaned again, " 'Let the Jews go free'!"

It seemed such a simple thing. Make a decree. Tell them all

to go home. Then forget it and go on with life.

But he couldn't bring himself to do it.

Suddenly he straightened up and clenched his fists, fury etched on his face. "Those people have been nothing but trouble for centuries," he growled. "They have a different God, different customs, a different day of worship." His mind conjured up sinister motives behind each of their peculiarities. "Why should I show them any special favors?"

He scowled as an evil image of savage Hebrews emerged within his brain. "Let them *rot* where they are!" he bellowed, his eyes narrowing. "I'm the *king* of Media-Persia—the *king* of Babylon. No one, *not even Daniel's God*, will tell *me* what to do!" His voice rose to thunderous tones as he hammered his fist on the table. "*I will not let them go!*"

Determination radiated from every pore. He rearranged his robes, wiped the sweat from his face, and strutted to the throne room, ready to hear the next case.

His iron resolve weakened within hours. The presence returned, whispering so insistently, "Open the gates," It said, "Let My people go."

More days of torture. More sleepless nights. Cyrus felt as though two supernatural forces fought hand to hand within his mind.

One power unleashed every evil impulse he'd ever known and filled his soul with darkness and despair. It tied his being into knots of hate and anger.

But the presence—It had sent cool drafts of love and peace blowing down the corridors of his soul. It had awakened the desire to bestow happiness upon his subjects—especially on the Jews.

How could he go on like this? He wanted possession of his own mind, but it seemed that one or the other of these superhuman powers would win the mastery. He had no choice, no escape. Even as a king, he must become a slave.

But which power would control him?

He struggled on. How long has it been? he wondered—nearly three weeks!

The face of Daniel floated up within his mind. What a man!

Kind, loving, intelligent—indispensable! He remembered the lions' den—described so graphically by Uncle Gobryas before he died. And he recalled other stories he'd heard from Babylonian merchants traveling in Persia years ago. Nebuchadnezzar's dreams. The fiery furnace. And—he didn't want to think of *that* now—Nebuchadnezzar's madness!

For twenty-one days, Cyrus resisted the presence. For twenty-one days he wavered between peace and horror, between love and hate, between sanity and madness.

At last he could hold out no more. Tears streamed down his cheeks as he surrendered to the presence. He wanted *peace* and *love* to rule his kingdom—not hate and anger. And he knew of no other way to receive it.

"Open the gates!" he shouted with joy. "Let God's people go back to their own country!"

The darkness and despair of three weeks of struggle vanished in an instant. Peace and joy that had hovered so fleetingly over and around him cascaded into his heart. Now he realized that in letting God's people go, he'd freed his own soul as well.

★　　　★　　　★　　　★

Daniel smiled as he entered the throne room and courteously bowed before Cyrus. "You've had a terrible struggle during the past weeks."

"You knew about it?"

"I prayed for you." The old prophet couldn't help sharing with his master the experience through which *he* had gone. "Gabriel—Yahweh's highest angel—sought to move your heart for three weeks, but you wouldn't move."

"An angel? The presence was an angel?"

"The more he pleaded with you, the more you resisted and the greater the effort of the evil one." Daniel put his finger to his temple. "It seemed that the evil one would win."

"I resisted something." Cyrus laughed. "I've never had such a battle in all my life."

"I knew that and continued to pray for you." Daniel studied the king's face. "But then a change took place. You decided that you wanted love. You chose to follow God. You put your will on His side."

"That must have been when I decided I wanted a kingdom of good instead of a kingdom of evil."

Daniel nodded. "But the evil one refused to leave. So Gabriel called to Yahweh for help."

"The strongest angel in heaven needed help?"

"The fight you couldn't see was far greater than the one that raged in your heart." The prophet's face became radiant. "When Gabriel called for help, Michael came to his aid. The Son of God flew to your side, and the evil one knew he'd lost."[6]

"The Son of God fought on my side?" Cyrus whispered the words, awed by the thought of so great a Person taking time to answer an old man's prayers. "I want Him to be on my side forever."

★   ★   ★   ★

The whole land filled with rejoicing as many of God's people prepared to return to Judah and rebuild Yahweh's temple. God had blessed His people. He had opened the gates, and now His people were free.

As they prepared for the journey, the Jews sang a song that someone had written for just this occasion:

"When the lord brought back the captives to Zion,
    we were like men who dreamed.
Our mouths were filled with laughter,
    our tongues with songs of joy.
Then it was said among the nations,
    'The Lord has done great things for them.'
The Lord has done great things for us,
    and we are filled with joy."[7]

---

1. See Jeremiah 25:11, 12.
2. Daniel 8:14, KJV.
3. Daniel 8:26.
4. Isaiah 45:13.
5. Isaiah 44:24–45:2, 13.
6. See Daniel 10:13.
7. Psalm 126:1-3.